Pedigreed Bloodlines

The Leigh Dennison Mysteries Series

Sandra Robbins

HEARTSONG
PRESENTS
MYSTERIES

To my mother, Maidelle Brundige, who gave me a love for reading and always supported my efforts.

To Susan Downs, thank you for believing in me. A special thanks to my critique partners Jess Ferguson, Marcia Gruver, Janelle Mowery, Lisa Ludwig, and Virginia Smith. To Kay Smith, Zann Wortham, Terry Jenkins-Brady, Tim Brady, and Chris Brinkley—my heartfelt gratitude for your support and friendship.

ISBN 978-1-59789-602-3

All scripture quotations are taken from the King James Version of the Bible.

All of the characters and events in this book are fictitious. Any resemblance to actual persons, living or dead, or to actual events is purely coincidental.

Cover Design: Kirk DouPonce, DogEared Design
Cover Illustration: Jody Williams

Our mission is to publish and distribute inspirational products offering exceptional value and biblical encouragement to the masses.

Printed in the U.S.A.

"They've got to be the best looking legs I've ever seen."

I must have said the words out loud. The two men who had just delivered a Queen Anne table to my antique shop stared at me as though I'd lost my mind. Perhaps I had. Excitement filled me that I could only compare to a combination of waking to gifts piled under the tree on Christmas morning and shooting Roman candles on the Fourth of July.

As the men exited with several backward glances, I stroked the graceful curve of the table's legs. Never in my wildest dreams would I have imagined owning such a masterpiece. Now here it sat in Dennison's Treasure Chest.

The events of the Asheville auction one week earlier were unclear except for the foggy recollection of smelling polished wood and competing with the bidders who sat around me. For the life of me, I had no idea how many times the auctioneer pointed to me, Leigh Dennison, the madwoman holding number twenty-five.

"And then they brought you out." My hand moved over the smooth surface. "I had to fight an all-out war to own you, but victory was never sweeter." My eyes closed as I relived the delicious moment. "Now you're all mine, you gorgeous piece of work."

A cough behind me yanked my mind back to the present. I turned around to face one of the deliverymen who had reentered the store.

"Uh, ma'am, are you okay?"

He glanced at the door then back to me as if deciding if he should bolt for safety.

I cleared my throat and straightened my shoulders in a pose that I hoped imitated the professional appraiser I saw from Christie's on the *Antiques Roadshow*. "I'm sorry. Just got carried away a little, that's all."

He pushed a clipboard toward me. "If you'll sign this, we'll get on out of here."

I scrawled my name on the delivery receipts. "Thanks for your help."

With a nod, the man grabbed the paper and headed for the door.

I stared after him. "They'll probably discuss the crazy lady they met all the way back to Asheville."

"Who are you talking to?"

"Uh, n–nobody." I whirled around at the voice of Marcie Payton, my best friend since childhood and my employee for the last year. She came toward me from the rear of the shop. "I didn't realize you were back from lunch."

Marcie headed to the counter, where the cash register sat, and laid her purse on a shelf underneath. "I'm later than I meant to be. Traffic was terrible like it always is this time of year."

Tourist season was just hitting its peak in the Smoky Mountains, and St. Claire, North Carolina, our little resort town, was flooded with visitors. Not only did they arrive en masse but they also brought their money with them. All the local residents realized if it weren't for people on vacation, we wouldn't have much business in our valley.

I glanced around the shop at the antiques for sale and thought of the woman who'd earlier purchased a nineteenth-century candle mold. "Well, their money does keep our town going."

"I know. And the sightseers will be gone soon, but by the end of winter I'll be eager for them to come back."

"Yeah, feast or famine. It's either tourist time or off-season, but I have to admit I love it."

"Me, too." She glanced down at the table for the first time. "So this is the purchase I've heard about all week. It's even more beautiful than you described."

I squatted down and pointed to my new prize. "Did you ever see such lovely cabriole legs? The out-curved knee and the incurved ankle are the best example of Queen Anne craftsmanship I've seen in a long time. I still can't believe I was able to get it."

Marcie crossed her arms and raised her eyebrows. "Oh no. Leigh Dennison, do I detect a hint in your voice that this piece won't be for sale?"

Marcie could read me like a book. She had already figured out my intentions. My face grew warm as I slowly stood and glanced around the shop. "I don't know," I murmured. "Now what did I do with that dust cloth?"

Marcie laid her hand on my arm and stopped me before I could make my escape. "You can't avoid the question that easily. Is this another piece that we're gonna be stuck with because you can't bear to sell it?"

I sank down into a Windsor rocker next to the table and caressed the glossy arms of the bow-spindle-backed chair. "It's not that I don't want to sell some of my pieces. It's just that I want the right person to appreciate them. You know. . .like I do."

Marcie shook her head, a little smile curling her lips. "Be careful, Leigh. You're gonna appreciate yourself right out of business. You opened this shop to sell antiques, but you're beginning to think of your inventory as your private collection."

"I know. But I can't let just *anybody* have them. I want Dennison's Treasure Chest to be dedicated to educating the public about our heritage. I'm just as interested in preserving the past as I am in selling what we have left of it."

Marcie sat down on the end of a Victorian fainting couch and leaned forward, her somber stare directed toward me. "I admit business has been good this summer. But as much as I hate to be the voice of reason that bursts your bubble, you've got to remember that winter is just around the corner. When it comes, the tourists leave. Then who's gonna buy your antiques?"

For the first time, doubt about my impulsive purchases crept into my mind. "Maybe I can sell some of the furniture I've been building in my workshop behind Addie's house."

"I don't understand it. You can focus so intently on a project when you're creating a reproduction of a table or a chair. What changes to make you so scatterbrained when you step into this store?"

I shot up out of the rocker, plopped down on the sofa beside Marcie, and sighed. "Do you think they're right?"

The puzzled look in her eyes told me she had no idea what I was talking about. "Who?"

"Our friends."

"Leigh, I'm not following you. What are you talking about?"

"Sarah and Mary. They say I remind them of their elementary school students who have ADD."

Marcie gave a little chuckle. "Oh, Leigh, you shouldn't pay attention to them."

The truth that I had been avoiding suddenly became clear. "They're right," I said. "I do have ADD. Maybe that's why I can't stay focused on something for a very long time."

Marcie waved her hand in dismissal. "I tell you all the time you're the smartest person I've ever known. Sarah and Mary are just jealous because you have a business."

Her words made sense, but then she majored in psychology in college. She'd certainly had plenty of opportunities to practice her skills on me. "Maybe you're right." I pushed up from the sofa. "You sure can make me feel better. I do have a business, and I need to get back to work."

Marcie reached out and grabbed my arm. "Speaking of the business, have you forgotten you have a payment due to Addie for the loan she gave you?"

Marcie might be able to make me feel better, but her no-nonsense attitude could bring me back to Earth in a hurry. "I haven't forgotten."

"Good. Then please don't go to any more sales and buy pieces that we may have to chop up for firewood this winter if we can't pay the electric bill."

The thought of my Queen Anne table being reduced to fuel for the fire made my stomach sink. But she was right about the loan payment to Addie Jordan. It was due in a month, and now guilt flooded over me because I'd spent everything I'd saved at the Asheville auction. I had no idea where I could come up with the money in the next few weeks, and I dreaded facing Addie, my seventy-year-old landlady and benefactress, with the truth.

Marcie started to say something, but the jingle of the bell above the entrance announced a customer. She glanced toward the front of the store and chuckled under her breath. "Well, it looks like your favorite schoolteacher just walked in."

As much as I wanted to, I couldn't turn around to look behind me. "Blake?"

"Prince Charming in the flesh."

Just the thought of Blake Cameron's penetrating dark eyes and black hair that tumbled across his forehead made my knees weak. The first time I saw him at church he was helping Emma Watkins, our oldest living member, down the front steps of the building after the service. Emma beamed as if she were royalty as Blake directed all his attention to her.

That's what I want, I thought. *A man who'll treat me like a queen.*

The more I got to know Blake, the more strongly I felt he was that man for me. Unfortunately, though, he seemed to think of me as his buddy at church—a volunteer with the youth group he taught and a member of his Tuesday night Bible study group. I rarely saw him anywhere else. Over the past year we had become friends, but much to my disappointment, it hadn't gone beyond that. Each Sunday I found myself studying him from my vantage point in the choir and hoping that one day he'd realize how much he wanted to know me better.

And now he was in my shop.

"What's he doing here? He's never come in here before."

"Why don't you ask him?"

Panic seized me. "I can't talk to him." I glanced down. "I look like I dressed in clothes from the missionary closet at church. I haven't even put on any makeup today. You wait on him."

A little grin pulled at Marcie's mouth. "My, my. How many times have I told you to dress better when you come to work? But do you ever listen to me?"

Hoping to straighten the wrinkles of my tee shirt, I pulled at its hem. "I was trying to be practical today. I wore these rags so I could clean the shop."

"You did it again, didn't you?" Marcie's crossed arms and raised eyebrows reminded me I couldn't hide anything from her.

She knows how I tend to let laundry pile up for a few days. Marcie doesn't understand how anyone can do this, and I couldn't tell her how I'd finally remembered to dump one load in the washer before falling into bed last night. Which led to my present predicament.

You see, I have a routine I follow every time I put clothes in the washer. Over and over I say to myself, *Put the soap in the washer. Put the soap in the washer.* It seems to work and keeps me from getting distracted by other things like getting a cup of coffee or going to check on the mail. That is, it works when I remember to do it.

On mornings when I'm running late, nothing is worse than pulling a load of wet clothes from the washer only to discover the machine ground its way through all the cycles without any detergent. And that's exactly what happened to me. With all my other clothes still lying on the laundry room floor, I had come to work dressed in jeans with a hole in the knee and a tee shirt that sported a big varnish stain across my midriff.

The desire to run out the back door overtook me, and I looked at Marcie, my chin quivering. "Please, help me."

Then Marcie—the one who nursed me through all my failed romances in high school, the one to whom I poured out my heart about my feelings for Blake—did a very wicked thing. She laughed and walked toward the back of the store and into the workroom, leaving me with my unwashed hair and unpainted lips to face the one man in the world for whom I would gladly rush into a burning house to rescue.

I swallowed, took a deep breath, and turned slowly. My legs wouldn't move as he sidestepped the furniture in the store and walked toward me. My heart pounded in my chest, the throbbing pulse in my neck beating like a drum. He stopped in front of me and smiled.

"Hi, Leigh. How're you today?"

My tongue, which seemed to possess a will of its own most of the time, suddenly chose that moment to cement itself to the roof of my mouth. "I'm—ah—I'm. . ."

The syllables coming from my mouth reminded me of when I was a child and tried to talk while eating a peanut butter and jelly sandwich. I concentrated on what I wanted to say and tried again. "I'm. . .I'm okay."

Now smile, a voice in my head commanded. My mouth curved upward, but he returned my smile and my heart starting pumping hard again.

"That's good." He shifted from one foot to the other and glanced around the shop. "Nice store."

"Thank you."

Coins jingled in his pocket the way my father's always did when he was lost in thought. "It's cool in here for such a hot day."

"Air conditioning, you know." Now that was a dumb answer. Of course he knew the shop was air-conditioned.

What was the matter with us? Our conversation so far sounded like an exchange between two five-year-olds. The coins in his pockets clinked together again, and he swallowed. A tiny drop of perspiration trickled down the side of his face, and it suddenly became clear. He was just as nervous and unsure of what to say as I was.

At the Tuesday night Bible study, he always seemed so composed and self-confident, and here he was in my shop looking like a high school boy trying to get up the nerve to talk to a girl. That thought calmed me, and I smiled, hoping it would put him at ease also.

"This is the first time I've seen you in here, Blake. Is there anything I can help you with?"

"Uh, yeah." His Adam's apple bobbed up and down. "I want to buy my mother a birthday present."

"Any idea what she'd like?" He couldn't seem to look me in the eyes.

He glanced around at the antiques displayed and reached for a Touraine flow-blue platter on the table next to where he stood. "Maybe this."

I tried to suppress a smile. "That's a good choice. The price on that piece is four hundred and fifty dollars plus tax." His eyes grew wide, and the blood drained from his face, leaving his summer tan as bleached as the sand I'd seen on my last trip to Myrtle Beach. His fingers began to shake, and I took the dish. "Do you want me to wrap it?"

The look of panic in his eyes reminded me of the rabbit that froze in the beam of my flashlight a few nights before when I surprised him in the vegetable garden. I struggled to keep from laughing out loud. More perspiration rolled down his face. "Uh, yeah, I guess so."

I didn't know why he was here, but from the look on his face, I knew it wasn't to buy a pricey antique. I set the platter down on the table and smiled at him. "You didn't come in here to buy a present for your mother. Why are you really here?"

His dark eyes stared into mine, and a sheepish grin tugged at the corner of his mouth. "To tell the truth. . ." He cleared his throat and tried again. "Actually, I came in to see you."

"Me?"

"Yeah. I've been trying to get my courage up for weeks to talk to you. Then when I finally do, I come in here and act like a complete idiot."

"Don't say that. You made my day. I haven't *almost* had such a big sale in a long time."

"I should have just told you why I came in the first place instead of trying to act like a big-shot antique buyer."

I shook my head. "No, I was impressed that you wanted to spend so much for your mother's birthday."

"Yeah, right. On a teacher's salary? I don't think so."

"Okay, so if you're not buying the platter, what did you come to see me about?"

He swallowed and blinked. "I want. . .I want. . .I want to ask you to have dinner with me."

Had I heard correctly? Blake Cameron was asking me for a date. I'd dreamed of this moment so many times, and now that it was here, I could only stand and stare at him mutely.

He stuck his hands back in his pockets, and the coins jingled again. "Of course, if you have other plans for tonight, I'll understand."

"No!" I almost clamped my hand over my mouth at my loud response. "I don't have plans. What time will you pick me up?"

A smile spread across his face. "Six thirty be okay?"

Still in shock, I nodded. "That's fine. I live out at Addie Jordan's farm. Do you know where that is?"

"Everybody knows where Addie's farm is. See you at six thirty."

With those words, he turned and walked out of the shop, leaving me standing next to my Queen Anne table, which suddenly didn't hold the allure it had earlier. Now my head was filled with thoughts of Blake Cameron and our upcoming dinner date.

I was wrong. He had noticed me at Bible study. A twinge of guilt pricked my conscience. Although I'd been a member of the group when Blake joined, I had to admit having him there made me look forward to Tuesday nights.

Now God was answering my prayer that Blake would notice me. It just reinforced what I'd always known. God loved me so much that He took care of me in every area of my life. I wrapped my arms around my body in satisfaction.

"Marcie," I called as I headed toward the workroom

at the back of the shop. "Don't stay in there pretending you didn't hear every word. Come on out. We're closing the shop early. I've got lots to do before Blake picks me up. This has got to be the best day of my life!"

S he'll be comin' round the mountain when she comes."

My truck tires hummed in rhythm with my singing as I traveled the winding road leading to the farm. What a beautiful day. The sun reflected off the rippling water of the shallow river that meandered through our mountain valley as I whizzed by, but my thoughts centered on one thing—dinner with Blake Cameron. Miracle of miracles, it finally happened, and I felt like I'd just been made Queen for a Day.

My mind was full of questions. Where will he take me? What should I wear? And then the most important question of them all. Did I remember to put soap in the washer and start the cycle again?

"Oh my. What clothes do I have clean?"

I felt so happy as I drove through the gates to the farm. A hanging sign announced to all passing by: JORDAN'S KENNELS, HOME OF CHAMPION NORWICH TERRIERS. White fences lined the driveway, which measured two-tenths of a mile from the entrance to the house. Memories of how lost I felt the day I drove up this gravel path toward my new home eight years ago washed over me. My life had changed since then, and it was all because of Addie Jordan.

The truck rounded a curve, and I gazed at the two-story colonial house, my home since my parents were killed in an auto accident when I was twenty years old and attending school at Duke. Addie, my mother's friend, embraced me during my time of grief. Her home became my refuge on school holidays and in the summers, and it seemed natural to come back home to her when I graduated. I had been here ever since, thanks to the business start-up loan she had fronted me.

How could I have spent the money intended for a payment to her? Knowing that Addie would forgive me when I told her only made my guilt worse. That's what made Addie so special. She gave so much love to so many people, and she never expected anything in return.

Sometimes I worried about her and the colorful characters she attracted. She never looked on the outside of a person. It was like she had Superman's X-ray vision, and she stared straight into a person's soul and met the needs she discovered there. She was one of a kind, and I loved her with all my heart.

I guided the car up the driveway and circled to the back of the house, pulling up in front of the kennels where Addie housed her prized dogs. A large SUV with a the magnetic sign on its door announcing in French script its owner—CELESTE'S CHAMPION NORWICH TERRIERS—sat in the driveway. Addie and Celeste stood next to the kennel gate in deep conversation.

Addie's face lit up as I stepped out of the truck, and she walked toward me, a straw hat covering her gray hair. "There's my girl! Home from another hard day at work. Sell anything today?"

"A candle mold. And I almost sold a flow-blue platter." I laughed and gave Addie a quick hug.

Celeste Witherington tilted her head to one side. The antique tortoiseshell combs that held her blond hair in place sparkled in the sunlight. Their shape and design were the most gorgeous I had ever seen. What I wouldn't give to have a set like them.

A vision of myself draped in a satin evening gown and cape, my long hair swept back and held in place by the combs, popped into my head. Like Cinderella on her way to the ball, I ascended the staircase toward my box seat at the opera to see *La Bohème*. Halfway up I paused and gave a regal nod to those in the theater lobby below. Admiration beamed from their upturned faces as they waved in return.

"*Bonjour*, Leigh." Celeste's voice interrupted my thoughts.

"Uh, hello, Celeste."

She cocked a pencil thin brow. "Addie tells me your shop is doing very well. I'm glad. We needed a quality shop in town. We have enough of those places that sell yard-sale rubbish."

"You'll have to come into the store sometime, Celeste."

"I will."

Addie stepped forward and looped her arm through mine. "Celeste came over to have a look at my dogs."

I smiled. "Want to see Addie's next champion, huh?"

Celeste's mouth turned up slightly at the corners. "*Oui, chérie.*"

"Well, enjoy your visit, Celeste. I'm sure Addie will be glad to give you any help you need."

Like how to produce a champion, I thought.

I smiled what I hoped was my most innocent expression and headed toward my workshop next to the kennels.

As I stepped inside the doorway to my woodworking shop, I stopped in surprise, my body stiff and my hands clenched at my sides. "What are you doing?"

The figure clothed in camouflage pants and a tee shirt turned to face me, and I took a step backward to distance myself from Preacher Cochran.

His shoulder-length brown hair, which he usually wore pulled back at the neck and held tight with a rubber band, stuck out beneath a cap that displayed the emblem of the North Carolina Tarheels. A scraggly beard did little to hide his facial scars, which Addie attributed to his exposure to Agent Orange in Vietnam. The man's appearance gave me a fright each time I saw him.

"I'm just lookin' around."

"How did you get in here?"

"Door wasn't locked."

His words jolted me. *Great. Now I'm forgetting to lock my shop.*

My gaze dropped to his hand, which grasped one of my antique woodworking tools, a prized mortise chisel. "Please put that back where it belongs."

He held it out to me. "I ain't gonna hurt it none. I just wanted to see what kind of tools you had."

I reached for the chisel. "In the future I'd appreciate

it if you'd stay out of here."

His shoulders drooped, and he let out a ragged breath. "Yeah, I will. You don't have to hit me over the head for me to know where I'm not wanted."

Preacher pushed past me, his shoulder brushing mine. I cringed. I had the same reaction each time I saw him. Addie felt differently, however. When she had heard earlier in the summer that a homeless Vietnam veteran had taken up residence underneath the bridge nearby, she went right over to see if he needed anything.

"He's just a man who's never recovered from that horrible war," she would often tell me, a faraway look in her eye. "I wonder sometimes if my son had survived would he have come home scarred for life like Preacher?"

I had no answer for Addie, because her son, her last living relative except for a distant cousin in Alabama, had come home from Vietnam in a body bag. Addie spoke little of her son, but tears often filled her eyes when she picked up her Bible, the last gift he gave her before he left for the jungles of Southeast Asia.

My attention turned back to the chisel as I examined it to see if he had damaged it. The handle, round and massive for such a delicate tool, fit snugly in the balled fist of my right hand, and I ran my left index finger down the tapering eight-inch blade. The metal, crafted by Isaac Greaves in England years before, gave the appearance of being fragile, but its sharp point could make quick work of gouging holes in even the hardest of woods.

With no damage apparent, I placed the chisel back in the display box above one of my workbenches. With everything in order, I headed back to the house. A quick glance around told me both Preacher and Celeste were gone.

A welcome sight greeted me as I entered the utility room of the house. The piles of my dirty laundry were gone from the floor, and stacks of neatly folded clothing lay in a basket on top of the dryer. My pressed pants, skirts, and blouses hung from wire hangers on the back of the door leading into the kitchen. Addie had come to my rescue again.

Voices drifted from the direction of Addie's office. I grabbed the basket of laundry and headed through the kitchen and toward the front of the house. As I approached her office door, the voices grew louder.

"Why can't you just leave me alone?"

The angry male voice brought me to a stop outside the partially open office door.

"Listen to me," Addie pleaded.

"No! Just get off my back! I don't need you meddling in my business."

Footfalls stomped across the floor, and the door flew open. Ross James, Addie's kennel employee, emerged, his dark eyes flashing. He glanced back into the study and then at me.

Without a word, he glared at me, brushed past, and hurried through the house and out the front door.

I clutched the basket of clothes tighter and stepped into the study. Addie stood behind her desk, her hands over her eyes.

"What happened?" I dropped the basket on the floor and hurried to her side. "Addie, are you all right?"

Addie straightened and wiped at her eyes. "I'm fine. I just had a little disagreement with Ross."

She sank down into the chair behind her desk, and I knelt beside her. "Why do you let that boy hang around here? Everybody in town says he's just trouble."

Addie shook her head. "No, he's not. He's just mixed up."

"But, Addie, that's no excuse to be disrespectful to you."

Addie looked at me with sadness in her eyes. "He's had some terrible things happen to him in his life."

"I know he dropped out of high school."

Addie clasped her hands on the desk and sighed. "The kids gave him a really hard time, Leigh. They called him a half-breed Cherokee and made fun of him because his father was known as the town drunk."

I put my arm around her shoulders. "His father was killed in a drunk-driving accident over at Black Mountain, wasn't he?"

"Yes, and Ross has taken care of his mother ever since. He needs this job to help her out."

"Well, I don't intend to have him speak to you that way again. I'll talk to him tomorrow. He's going to apologize for how he acted."

She shook her head. "No need for that, Leigh. It'll be all right."

I squeezed her shoulder in a quick hug. "You're too good for your own good, Addie. I don't want to see you get hurt because you trust the wrong people."

Addie turned to me, and in her eyes I saw concern, not for Ross but for me. She cupped my face in her hands. "Don't worry about me. Just remember what I've told you. You don't need to try to preserve the past when there are so many people in the present who need help."

Her words, so familiar, caused me to smile. I stood up. "I know. You tell me that often enough, but you'll have to continue working on me after I get back from my big date tonight."

"Date? Who with?" Addie jumped up from her chair, her face beaming.

My excitement of earlier returned, and I grabbed Addie in another hug. "None other than Mr. Blake Cameron, the one I thought hardly noticed me at all."

A little squeal escaped Addie's lips. "Well, it's about time he caught on to how special you are. I couldn't be happier."

"Thanks, Addie. I knew you'd be excited for me."

Addie sat back down at her desk and glanced up at me. "You know there are several reasons I like Blake."

"Like what?"

Addie leaned back in her chair and laced her fingers. "First and foremost, he's a believer. I always enjoy seeing him in church on Sunday. Second, he has a good job. And third," she said, pausing as if to whet my interest, "but very importantly, he's a dog lover."

Now this was a surprise. "How do you know that?"

A smile spread across her face. "Oh, I see him around town in his truck with his big, red bloodhound riding in the back. Sometimes the dog's inside with his head sticking out the window. You gotta love a man who treats his animals well."

"Really? I don't think I've ever seen the dog. Surely he won't bring it tonight."

"You never can tell." A teasing grin lined her face as she opened the desk drawer and pulled out the bank bag, which held the kennel's undeposited receipts for the month. Checks and currency tumbled from the unzipped bag onto the top of the desk.

"Let me help. I'll add the checks and endorse them while you count the money."

For several minutes, we worked silently until the deposit was complete. "You've brought in a lot of money with the sale of that last litter."

Addie zipped the moneybag closed and sighed before she looked at me. "Leigh, you like my dogs, don't you?"

"Why sure, Addie. I just haven't been around to help with them much, but I'll have more time once tourist season is over. I can leave Marcie at the shop to close up so I can come home early."

She shook her head. "No, that's not necessary as long as I have Ross. I just had to know if you liked them and would always make sure they were taken care of."

Her words sent off an alarm in my mind. "Addie, you're not sick or anything, are you?"

She laughed. "No, nothing like that. I just wondered. But there is something I need to talk to you about." She glanced at her watch. "But it can wait. Go get ready for your date."

I reached for the moneybag. "Do you want me to put this in the night box at the bank when we go out?"

"No, it can wait until tomorrow."

I picked up the basket and started for the door but stopped. "And thank you for doing my laundry. You're the best."

"Go on now." She pushed the moneybag to the side of her desk, picked up her latest dog magazine, and began to flip through the pages.

Two hours later, I sat on the front porch in the wicker swing waiting for Blake to arrive. At the first sight of his late-model white Ford truck, I stood up and studied the vehicle. To my relief no bloodhound rode in the front seat.

My heartbeat quickened as Blake stepped out of the truck and walked toward the porch. His dark hair, neatly combed in place, and his piercing brown eyes stirred feelings in me I had never experienced before. His creased khakis rustled as he walked, and the fabric of his blue knit shirt stretched across his muscular chest and shoulders. But it was his smile that held me spellbound. His lips drew back, revealing his perfect teeth.

"You must have had a great orthodontist."

He halted, his foot poised on the first step. "What?"

Whatever possessed me to say that? My tongue was taking over again. "What I meant is, your teeth are so perfect, you must have spent a lot of time at the dentist."

"Really?"

My face burned like fire. "Not that I think you had crooked teeth. It's just that they look like they've had a lot of work done on them."

This wasn't the opening conversation I had imagined with Blake. Any minute I expected him to turn around, jump in his truck, and roar down the driveway, never to return.

Blake stared at me for a moment, and laughed. "You have the greatest sense of humor of anyone I've ever met. That's what caught my attention at Bible study. I never know what's going to come out of your mouth next."

"Neither do I." I wrapped my fingers around the chain holding the swing and tried to focus on saying something intelligent.

"I hope I didn't keep you waiting."

"You didn't. I thought I was going to be late myself. The time got away from me while I was helping Addie with her bank deposit."

His gaze traveled over me. "Are you ready to go? I have reservations at the Silver Spoon for seven o'clock."

The Silver Spoon—the swankiest restaurant this side of Asheville? The black sundress with spaghetti straps I wore was a perfect choice. Almost perfect, I realized with a start. There was one problem. I had meant to bring the matching jacket in case the restaurant was too cool. The jacket, instead of covering my shoulders, still lay on my bed.

I reached behind me and groped for the doorknob. "I forgot something. Go on and get in the truck, Blake. I'll just be a minute."

I ran back into the house and flew up the staircase in the entry hall. Inside my bedroom the jacket still lay where I had placed it earlier. As I jerked it on, my reflection in the mirror caught my attention.

"I need more lipstick."

The dresser drawer that held my cosmetics picked this time to refuse to open, and I tugged with all my might. It tumbled with a crash to the floor, scattering all the contents.

"What a time for this to happen. I don't have time to clean up this mess."

I groaned and dropped to my knees then scooped up the cosmetics and dumped them back in the drawer. I grabbed my lipstick and faced the mirror. "Why does everything go wrong when I'm in a hurry?"

The black sandals I'd been saving for a special occasion thumped as I raced down the staircase. I paused at the bottom and looked toward the closed door to Addie's study. I started to go in but then glanced toward the front of the house. A handsome young man waited for me. I resisted the urge to tell Addie good night and headed outside.

Dinner with Blake turned out to be everything I had ever imagined. From the minute we walked in the door, I was captivated. The smell of baking bread sent an aroma through the room that made my stomach growl. Waiters in white coats stood beside tables and served plates filled with the most delicious looking food I'd ever seen. A maitre d' held my chair for me as he seated us at a table beside a window overlooking the Little Pigeon River.

Before I knew what was happening, waiters appeared to welcome us, pour water, and give us menus. Making a decision on what to order was hard. There were too many options. I finally gave up and let Blake choose.

The candles on the table, the gleaming silver goblets and china, and the attention of the staff, made the evening the most special of my life. As I swallowed the last bite of the southern pecan pie I'd ordered for dessert, I glanced around at the gorgeous prints on the wall. All depicted a scene in the Smokies—the view from Clingman's Dome, an 1800s church in Cades Cove with a background of the surrounding mountains, autumn foliage across Newfound Gap, and various scenes shot on hiking trails.

All of this and Blake's company combined to make the night one of the best memories ever.

"What a classy place! I'm not used to waiters putting your napkin in your lap and brushing crumbs away every time you take a bite. They don't do that at the Dairy Bar."

Blake's chuckle turned into laughter. "Oh, Leigh, you crack me up. Every Tuesday night I go home from

Bible study and laugh at all the funny things you said."

"Really?"

A muscle twitched in his jaw. "Yeah. You seem so confident and sure of yourself. I've been wanting to ask you out for a long time, but I didn't think you'd go out with me."

"But why not?"

He shrugged. "I don't know. I've never had much of a social life outside of school and church. I'm just a quiet guy who loves kids. I can't see myself ever doing anything but teaching. I feel like that's what God called me to do."

"But I think teaching is a noble profession."

"Noble. Could be." He tilted his head. "But the monetary rewards—"

"Ever since I saw a rerun on TV of Sidney Poitier in *To Sir, with Love*. . . The way he turned those kids' lives around was amazing. And the ending, when he encountered a boy and girl who were so disrespectful, he knew his work there wasn't finished. That was awesome."

He smiled. "You liked that movie? It's one of my favorites. I'll bet there's not another woman in St. Claire who's seen it. I'm just glad I don't have to deal with the kind of troubled students he did."

Blake reached for his water, and I noticed his hand shook. Just as he picked up the glass, it slipped from his fingers and tipped. He grabbed for it and caught it before it spilled on the table. He wrapped both hands around the goblet and steadied it.

The near mishap startled me. "Is something wrong?"

"Sorry," he said. "Don't get me wrong. I love teaching, but sometimes I wish I made more money. Then I could help my parents more."

"What do you mean?"

He set down the glass then looked at me. "They're having trouble paying for some expensive medical tests my father had."

The sad look in his eyes pricked my heart. "Oh, Blake, I'm so sorry."

He took a deep breath, straightened in his seat, and smiled. "We don't need to be talking about my problems. Not when I'm enjoying being with you so much."

"This has been a wonderful evening. Thank you, Blake."

He folded his napkin and laid it beside his plate but hesitated a moment before he looked at me. "Do you think you'd go out with me again?"

Steady, girl. Don't let him see how excited you are. This is not a marriage proposal, just another date.

"I'd like that. But I guess I should warn you. I have this problem."

"A problem, huh?"

"Yes. For some reason I never know what I'm going to say next. You may find that irritating."

He swallowed before he answered. "I think you're wonderful. Maybe tonight's going to be the beginning of a new friendship for us both."

"I'd like that."

He met my gaze and smiled. "But please don't expect me to bring you back to this place very often.

It's a little rich for my blood."

I glanced around at the décor of the dining room. Dim rays of light from the crystal chandeliers filtered across the candlelit tables. This place would always have a special meaning for me because Blake had been the one to bring me here. But I realized that his presence was really what made the evening for me. It didn't matter where I ate as long as he was there.

"Mine, too. I'm pretty easy to please. Pizza and hamburgers suit me fine."

"Me, too." He picked up his napkin and dabbed at the perspiration dotting his forehead. Then he bit his lip, glanced around the room, and motioned for the waiter to bring the check.

It had turned out to be a wonderful evening, but a nagging thought troubled me. At times throughout the meal, Blake had appeared extremely nervous. The spilled water and the perspiration in such a cool room bothered me. Perhaps it was first date jitters and concern for his parents. . .

Don't look for trouble. Blake wants to ask you out again.

I sank back in my chair, picked up my coffee cup, and drained the last drop.

———

We chatted all the way home about our jobs, the Bible study class, a mission project that we were planning at church, and a myriad of other topics. The conversation was easy, and I wondered if Blake felt the bond growing between us that I sensed. It was too early to know for sure, but I believed the best for us was yet to come.

As we rounded the curve of the driveway, the house came into view, and I felt uneasy. Usually, the house with its lights ablaze at night always stood like a beacon in the darkness of the countryside. But not on this night.

"That's odd," I said.

Blake glanced over at me. "What?"

"The window to Addie's office is lit, but there are no lights on in the rest of the house."

"Maybe she's already gone to bed," Blake offered as we got out and walked up onto the porch.

I shook my head, my legs suddenly leaden. "No. Addie wouldn't go to bed without hearing about my evening. What if she's sick?"

"You're getting yourself upset over nothing." Blake swung open the front door. "Come on. I'll go in with you."

We stepped into the entry hall. "Addie, where are you?"

My voice echoed through the silent house, and I headed toward the closed door to her office. I knocked, lightly at first. "Addie, are you in there?"

No answer came. I knocked harder, grasped and turned the knob, and then pushed the door open a crack. "Addie? It's me, Leigh."

"She's probably in her room asleep," Blake whispered.

I forced a smile. "Probably," I said, pushing the door open wide.

My gaze swept the room. Settled on the stained carpet. I opened my mouth. A silent scream caught in my throat.

In front of me, sprawled facedown on the floor, lay the woman I loved like a mother. Blood soaked her white silk blouse and covered the carpet around her still form.

I stood stone-still, trying to make sense of the scene. "Help!" I mouthed the word, realized I was hanging onto Blake's arm to keep my balance. Had she fallen? Hit her head? Blake was speaking. His words were a rushing sound through my ears. I turned back to Addie. And then I saw it. The handle of my antique mortise chisel protruded from her back.

A scream tore from my throat. I ran forward, dropped to my knees next to her. Blake followed and knelt on the other side.

My fingers searched for the pulse in her neck, but I found nothing. Tears blurred my vision as I stared at Blake. "Addie. She's dead."

eigh, are you all right?" Marcie's voice drifted across the room from the doorway. "Leigh?"

I glanced up from the kitchen chair where I sat, my hands clasped on top of the table. I tried to answer, but no words came.

Marcie walked across the room and sat beside me. "You're not alone. I'm here with you."

A little sob caught in my throat. "Did you see her, Marcie?"

"No, but Blake told me."

Marcie reached out and grasped my hands. For several minutes, we sat in silence, tears rolling down my face. Finally, I reached for a napkin that Addie always kept in the holder in the middle of the table and dried my eyes. "Where's Blake?"

"He's with the police in the study."

"Addie's dead, Marcie." I wiped at the fresh tears that trickled down my face. "I've lost my second mother."

Marcie bit her lip. "I know."

"Who would do such a thing?"

"I don't know. The police want to talk to you when you're up to it. Do you feel like it now?"

"Yes." I started to get up, but Marcie stopped me.

"I'll tell them to come in here. You don't need to go back in the study just yet. The coroner's in there."

"This is a nightmare. Please wake me up." I grabbed Marcie's hands and squeezed.

Tears formed in Marcie's eyes. "I'm sorry, Leigh. I know this has been a terrible shock for you. But I'll be with you as long as you need me."

She turned and walked from the room. My glance darted around the four walls, and I rubbed my clammy palms on my skirt. I imagined the walls shrinking inward, closing me into a lonely prison. I pushed out of the chair, stumbled to the window, and pressed my hands to the glass.

My head dipped and touched the pane, which shielded me from the night. "I'm really alone now."

"Excuse me, Miss Dennison. I'm Detective John Sawyer with the St. Claire Police Department. I'd like to ask you a few questions if you feel up to it."

A man stood behind me. Perhaps in his midthirties, he wore navy pants and a red shirt with the initials SCPD monogrammed on the pocket. A gold badge, fastened to the left side of his belt buckle, gleamed in the overhead light. A handgun in a holster hung on the right.

I walked back and sat down. "Yes. Please tell me what happened."

He walked toward me and slumped in the chair Marcie had vacated. He pulled a small notepad and pen from his pocket and looked at me. "Why don't you start by telling me what you remember?"

His noncommittal expression didn't change as I recalled the events of the day. His fingers holding the pen flew across the page as I talked.

He stopped writing when I told him about seeing Preacher Cochran with the mortise chisel in my shop. "And what did you do with the chisel?"

"I put it back in the case."

Detective Sawyer wrote something else. "Did you lock the door when you left?"

I rubbed my forehead, trying to force a memory. "I don't remember. I was going out for the evening, and I was in a hurry." Try as I might I couldn't remember locking my shop. The terrible truth hit me. I'd been too distracted thinking about my date. I reached for another napkin and wiped at my eyes. "I didn't lock up. And now Addie's dead."

He wrote something else on his pad. "Please go on."

When I finished, he looked over his notes and then flipped several pages back. He studied what he'd written before he glanced up at me. "So the last time you saw Mrs. Jordan was when you went upstairs to get ready?"

"That's correct."

"But before you left her, you helped her with a bank deposit?"

"Yes. It was on her desk when I left."

"Well, there's no deposit there now."

My breath caught in my throat. "Do you think the killer took the money? Was that the motive?"

He shrugged. "We don't have any theories yet. We're just collecting information."

The memory of Addie's argument with Ross

James crossed my mind. "Have you talked to Addie's employee Ross James? She told me he was having a hard time financially since he dropped out of school. That's why she gave him a job."

"We haven't located him yet," the policeman murmured.

I frowned at this unexpected information. "You mean he's disappeared?"

"Did he drive Mrs. Jordan's truck home in the evenings?" he asked, ignoring my question.

I shook my head. "Of course not. Addie's truck should be in the garage next to the kennel."

The detective stared into my face. "It's not there. Louie down at the gas station told one of our officers that Ross James filled Addie's truck up with gas about seven thirty, paid him with cash, and drove off. Have any idea where he might have gone?"

The detective's words made no sense to me. It sounded like Addie's murder was developing into a case you might see on my favorite television shows. "Let me get this straight. Addie's money, truck, and her employee are missing. There's something terribly wrong here."

Detective Sawyer glanced down at the pad again. "Maybe. But I can't jump to any conclusions."

"Have you put out a missing persons bulletin on Ross?"

"No."

I jumped up from the chair. "Why not? Lt. Green on *Law and Order* would realize he's the chief suspect right away and try to find him."

Detective Sawyer sighed and looked upward. "Oh, you're an armchair detective, huh?"

"No," I sputtered. "But you need to do something… like, uh, like take a Code Seven."

He frowned. "You want me to go to lunch?"

"What do you mean by that?"

"Miss Dennison, taking a Code Seven means a policeman's going to lunch."

I was doing it again. Reacting before I had time to think. But this was different. A killer was escaping, and the police didn't seem concerned enough do to anything about it. "Well, you have to do something to find Ross. How about notifying Amber Alert?"

The look on his face told me he thought I'd lost my mind. "Amber Alert is only for abducted or missing children. I don't think that applies in this case."

"Then what are you going to do?" I paced back and forth in front of him.

He cleared his throat. "Don't worry. We'll find Ross. Now why don't you sit back down? I have just a few more questions for you, and then I'll leave you alone."

"Okay," I said as I dropped into the chair. "What else can I tell you?"

"Now you said after you helped with the deposit you went upstairs. Then you came down and waited on the porch until Mr. Cameron arrived?"

"Yes."

"And then you left for dinner?"

"Yes."

He leaned forward, his eyes narrowed. "Well, according to Mr. Cameron, when he arrived, you had to go back inside, and you were gone for several minutes."

What a time to lose my focus. I closed my eyes and rubbed my temples with my fingertips. "Oh, I forgot about that. I had to go back and get my jacket. I was only gone for a few minutes."

"Well, it only took a few minutes for someone to kill Addie Jordan."

His menacing words shocked me, and I sprang from the chair again. "Surely you don't think I killed Addie!"

The detective stood up, closed his notebook, and stared at me. "I'm not accusing anybody right now. I'm just saying that you, along with several others, are a person of interest in our investigation. Don't plan on leaving town or anything like that until this case is closed."

I could hardly believe my ears.

He stopped, stuck his pen in his monogrammed shirt pocket, and smiled. "We'll be in touch."

I stood in stunned silence as he walked from the room. How could anyone think I could kill the woman I loved like a mother?

The events of the afternoon replayed in my mind from the time I came home until I left for dinner with Blake. Addie was alive when I left her in the study, and I assumed she was when I'd gone back upstairs. I should have opened that door and told her good-bye when I came back down after getting my jacket. But at the time, my mind was focused on Blake, and. . .

My thoughts froze in mid-sentence. At dinner Blake said his parents needed money, and Addie's bank deposit was missing. He'd been at the bottom of the porch steps when I left and when I came back down. He would have had time to go inside and kill Addie. Could he be one of the persons of interest in the case? I shook my head in denial. Not Blake. But still, he was alone for the entire time I was upstairs. And he was so fidgety all through dinner.

"Are you okay?"

I jumped at the sound of Blake's voice from the doorway. I turned to face him. "I'm not sure. The policeman told me I'm a person of interest in the case. How could he think that?"

Blake stuck his hands in his pockets, walked into the room, and stopped beside me. "Don't worry about that. He told me the same thing. They have to follow every lead without prejudice."

I was right. Blake is a suspect, too.

I shook my head. I couldn't think that way. "But it's as clear as the nose on my face. Ross James killed Addie and stole her money and truck. Why can't they see that? They need to find him as quickly as they can."

"Leigh, I've known Ross ever since he started high school. I can't believe he would commit murder. I had him in one of my English classes, and he helped design the scenery for one of our plays. I thought he showed great promise. That's why I was so concerned when he dropped out of school. I kept hoping he'd finish his diploma."

"I'm afraid I've never been able to recognize the good qualities that you and Addie saw in Ross."

Blake's face turned red. "Maybe you've never looked for them."

I crossed my arms and stared at him. "Yeah, they were really evident this afternoon when he was yelling at Addie. I don't know why she ever thought. . ." A howl from the direction of the kennels interrupted me. "What's that?"

Blake went to the window and peered out into the darkness. "It's the dogs. They're barking again. I went down and checked on them a little while ago. They seemed fine, but they're very agitated."

"They must sense something's wrong. They loved Addie so much."

The distress I heard in the howls from the kennel touched my heart. I had never paid much attention to the dogs, but now they were just as lost without Addie as I was. "What's going to happen to them? I don't know anything about taking care of those dogs. But somebody will have to do it until arrangements can be made for them."

Blake rested his hand on my shoulder. "If you'd like, I'll see that they're fed and cared for until we know who'll inherit them."

I felt guilty for what I'd been thinking. He wasn't a murderer. He was just as wonderful as I thought the first time I saw him. "Thanks, Blake. Addie told me you were a dog lover. She liked that about you." I smiled through my tears. "She would be happy to know you're going to care for them for a while. But I'll help you."

Marcie walked back into the room at that moment. "The police are going to be here for a while. Leigh, I want you to pack a few clothes. You're going home with me for the night. As soon as the police tell us it's okay, I'll get a cleaning service to come clean the study. But until then, I don't think you need to stay here."

The news that I had somewhere else to stay that night calmed me. Marcie and I went upstairs to pack my overnight bag. As I placed the clothes Addie washed and folded into my suitcase, I had to stop several times to wipe away the tears.

When I finished, I drove over to Marcie's. The headlights from Blake's truck in my rearview mirror raised conflicting thoughts. Was he really what he appeared to be, or was he instead a murderer?

———

Over the next few days, Blake and I worked together to care for the dogs living in the kennel. Addie only bred her best parent dogs, and at the present time the kennel housed Bud and Teenie, whose litter had been sold, and Beau and Belle, along with their prized puppy Macris Labelle Beaumont III. Try as I might, I couldn't remember the nickname Addie had given him.

Three mornings after the murder I stood at the

fence and watched Blake as he fed the stocky, little dogs that had been the love of Addie's heart. Their spirited and playful nature was evident as they jumped on Blake and rested their paws on his shins.

He looked at me and laughed. "These dogs are great. They're a lot smaller than my bloodhound."

"Yeah. Addie said they're one of the smallest of the working terriers but that they had big hearts to make up for their little bodies."

Blake dropped down and cupped Belle's face in his hand. "Look at that foxy expression, Leigh. And their wiry coat and these prick ears."

Out of the corner of my eye, I spotted their puppy several feet away and pointed to him. "He doesn't seem so happy, though."

Blake stood and looked toward where the puppy lay on his stomach, his head resting between his outstretched paws. His perky ears drooped, and his little body trembled.

His sad eyes stared up as Blake squatted beside him. "I think he misses Addie."

"Could be. She had great hopes for him, you know. Time after time, she told me how only once in a lifetime does a breeder produce a dog that conforms to its breed's standard with such accuracy as this puppy. She thought she finally had a shot at the Best in Show trophy from the Westminster Dog Show in New York."

"Maybe whoever buys him will want to follow Addie's dream."

I leaned against the fence and studied the puppy.

"I have to admit I haven't worked with the dogs much, but they're not as playful as I've seen them in the past. All of them seem so subdued this morning. I think I'll have Addie's veterinarian come take a look at them."

Blake scooped the puppy up and walked to the fence. "That's a good idea. You know Dr. Miller retired to Florida last month. There's a new vet in town."

I glanced at him in surprise. "I didn't know. What's the new vet's name?"

Blake's brow furrowed. "Um, it starts with a *B*, I think. Brown? No." His eyes lit up. "Baker, that's it. Dr. Baker."

I reached out and gave the puppy a tentative pat. "Well, Dr. Baker's never seen the dogs, but I'm sure he'll be okay."

"Sure. He'll know if anything is physically wrong with them. But I've read that dogs are very sensitive. They know when something's wrong. I'm sure they'll eventually return to normal." Blake scratched the puppy on the nape of the neck. His body shivered, and his eyes peered up as Blake continued to stroke him.

Something in that movement puzzled me. "Return to normal? I don't know if that will ever happen. I can't sleep at night because the police haven't arrested anybody, and as far as I know, Ross James hasn't been located."

"I'm sure they're working on it." He glanced up at me. "How are you making it over at Marcie's?"

I looked over my shoulder at the house I'd called home for the past eight years. "I miss Addie and being here with her. I guess I'd better get used to it, though. I won't be able to live here with whoever inherits the farm and kennel. And I have no idea what will happen to Addie's beloved dogs. How can things change so much in a few days?"

Blake put the puppy down and walked from the kennel. As he started to close the gate, he frowned. "This lock is broken. I'll get that fixed first thing in the morning."

I hadn't even noticed the lock, but I was thankful Blake had. Addie would have seen it right away.

Blake looked at me. "Are you ready for the funeral tomorrow?"

I wanted to forget the funeral, but that was impossible. "I suppose so."

"I'll be there for you tomorrow, too."

I buried my suspicions under a shaky smile. "Thanks."

～

The tree-covered mountains that towered around our valley had never appeared more majestic than they did on the day of the funeral. The sanctuary, filled with flowers, was crowded to capacity with friends from the area, and many traveled great distances to be there.

Pastor William Franklin delivered a eulogy befitting the gracious lady who lay in state before us. He recited from the book of Proverbs, "Who can find a virtuous woman?" As he read the characteristics of such a woman, I knew Addie had embodied each one of them.

At the grave site, I kissed the tips of my fingers, touched the casket, and placed a rose atop it. With Blake and Marcie at my side, I greeted the mourners as I made my way toward the car supplied by the funeral home.

I stopped as I caught sight of Detective Sawyer standing off to the side of those assembled. He nodded my way, and I returned the greeting before Blake took my arm and guided me toward the car.

Silence surrounded us all the way back to the church where Blake had parked his truck.

"Want to go out to Addie's with me to feed the dogs?" he asked as we got into his vehicle.

The black silk skirt and jacket I wore clung to me from the heat in the cemetery. I could hardly wait to get out of it and into a pair of jeans, but the dogs had to be cared for. "I guess so. I need to get more clothes, and I can change while we're there."

His gaze drifted over my face. "Want to go out to eat tonight?"

"I don't think so. Why don't you come back to Marcie's with me? The three of us can order a pizza."

The minute we drove into the yard, I could hear the dogs howling, just as they had done ever since Addie's death. I was ready for them to stop.

I watched from outside the kennel while Blake fed and watered them. Beau and Belle ran to the food bowls, but the puppy headed toward Blake. With a laugh, Blake picked him up and patted him. "I think he likes me." He walked over to the fence and held him up for me to see. "Now isn't that the cutest face you ever did see?"

The puppy peered at me, and I reached through the fence to pat him. A memory of Addie holding him flashed into my mind. "Addie sure loved you, Labelle."

"Labelle? That's a big name for such a little fellow." Blake glanced back at Beau and Belle as they trotted away from the food bowl. "Your turn," he said as he deposited the puppy on the ground.

Blake stepped from the pen, fastened the lock that he'd repaired earlier, and leaned against the fence. We stood there until the puppy ate his fill and trotted away. Beau and Belle didn't move as Labelle lay down beside them.

I glanced at the back of the house. "Do you mind going in with me while I get my clothes?"

"Sure thing."

Once inside the house I hesitated outside the closed door to the study. The crime scene tape across the entrance served as a grim reminder of what had transpired inside that room. I turned away and moved on to the staircase in the entry.

I stopped at the foot of the stairs. "Wait for me here. I'll just be a few minutes. I want to get. . . What's that?"

Blake headed toward the front door. "A car just stopped in the driveway. Were you expecting anyone?"

"No. Maybe Marcie decided to come out here to help."

Blake opened the door with me right behind him. He took a step onto the porch and stopped. "Where have you been?"

I nudged Blake onto the porch and stepped around him. My breath caught in my throat at the sight before me. Ross James, a big smile on his face, climbed from Addie's truck and walked toward us. "Hey, Mr. Cameron. What're you doing here?"

Blake glanced at me and took a step forward. "Ross, everybody's been trying to find you."

A look of alarm crossed Ross's face. "Is it my mother? Has something happened to her?"

"No, it's not your mother," Blake said.

"Then what is it?"

Blake started to speak, but he stopped and turned to me. "Leigh, why don't you call Detective Sawyer?"

How I wanted to charge across the porch, grab Ross by the shoulders, and shake him until I was exhausted, but Blake's hand restrained me. Every night since Addie's death, I had relived the conversation I'd overheard between him and Addie, and I wanted to make him pay for the hateful words.

Instead of giving in to my emotions, I turned away, pulled my cell phone from my jacket pocket, and dialed the police station. With the call completed, I rejoined Blake and Ross.

"The police will be here in a few minutes."

The boy sat beside Blake in the swing, his fingers wrapped around the chain. His eyes clouded when he looked up at me. The rhythmic creak of the swing resonated across the porch as I studied Ross's face in hopes of seeing sorrow, remorse, or some emotion. But there was nothing I could detect except that same defiance I had seen when he stormed past me out of Addie's office.

Ross glanced down at the floor and then back to me. "Miss Dennison, I'm sorry about Mrs. Jordan."

"Are you sorry, Ross?"

His eyes narrowed, and he stood to face me. "I didn't kill her if that's what you mean."

"I heard you arguing with her, and then you disappeared."

Ross jammed his hands in his pockets. "I didn't run away. Miss Addie gave me the money to go on a trip. She even told me to use her truck."

"Why would Addie do something like that?"

Ross looked at Blake and then jerked his head toward me. "She's never liked me, you know. But Miss Addie was a different story. She's been after me to learn more about my ancestors, the Cherokee. I thought she was crazy. She said I was throwing my life away after I dropped out of school."

Ross paused for a moment, and Blake pushed up from the swing. "Go on."

"Well, there's not much else to the story. She gave me some money and told me to take her truck over to Cherokee for a few days. She said my people had a great history, and I needed to realize I was wasting my heritage."

"So you went?" Blake asked.

"I didn't want to at first. In fact, we had a terrible argument. I told her to quit meddling in my life, but then I cooled off and thought about what she said. I went back later and apologized. She told me to go on and take a few days off, so I did."

This tale was beginning to grate on my nerves. "That's quite a story, Ross. Did you steal the money after you killed her?"

Ross whirled around to face me, his fists clenched. His eyes shot sparks of hatred at me. "I didn't steal her money, and I didn't kill her!" He took a step toward me. "But maybe *you* did. I know all about the money Miss Addie loaned you. Maybe you didn't want to pay it back."

"Wh–what? How do you. . ." His words spoken with such fury shocked me to the point I couldn't speak.

He advanced toward me. "I heard you and Miss Addie talking about all the money she gave you for that fancy shop of yours. You found yourself a gold mine when you moved in here, didn't you?"

Blake stepped beside Ross and grasped his arm. "That's enough, Ross. Leigh's had a rough time the past few days. You can't speak to her that way."

Ross tore his eyes away from me and looked at Blake. He started to speak but seemed to waver at the expression on Blake's face. "Sorry, Mr. Cameron."

Ross turned his back on us and walked to the edge of the porch. Blake and I stood in silence as we waited for the police to arrive. I breathed a sigh of relief when the black and white cruiser came into view. Detective Sawyer and a younger man in uniform stepped out of the car and walked up the steps to the porch.

Detective Sawyer acknowledged us with a nod then turned to Ross. "Hello, Ross. Decided to come home, huh?"

"I can explain."

"You can do that at the station." He pointed to the police car. "Why don't you get in?"

Blake stepped forward. "Is Ross under arrest?"

Detective Sawyer's face gave no hint of what he was thinking. "We just need to question him right now. And we're going to need to examine the truck. Our lab guys are on their way to check it out now."

The uniformed officer held the back door of the car open for Ross. Then he and Detective Sawyer climbed in and drove away.

I stood on Addie's front porch and stared after the car. How could the police be blind to Ross James's involvement in Addie's murder?

"I can't believe they didn't arrest him."

Blake frowned. "And I can't believe Ross would hurt anybody. You have to let the police do their job. They'll find Addie's killer."

"I'm beginning to doubt that."

He stared at me, a hurt look flickering in his eyes. "I'll go put up the dogs for the night." Blake trudged down the steps, stuck his hands into his pockets, and walked toward the kennel.

Why was he so certain that Ross was innocent? Could it be because he knew the guilty person?

Within minutes, Blake reappeared at the corner of the house. "The dogs weren't too happy when I left them." He stared up at me standing on the porch. "Leigh, I know this has been a terrible ordeal for you."

Before I could respond, the sound of barking came

from the kennel. I pressed my hands over my ears. "I want to go to Marcie's house and forget everything that's happened. I have to figure out what I'm going to do."

"What do you mean?"

"I've lived here ever since my parents died. Their house was sold years ago. Now I'll have to leave this one, too." Pain radiated through my head, and I rubbed my hand across my forehead in an effort to stave off a headache. "I just feel lost, Blake."

He climbed the porch steps and stopped beside me. "Maybe things will look better in the morning."

Before I could answer him, the phone inside rang. I stared at the front door, not wanting to reenter the house. Blake must have read my mind.

"I'll get that for you," he said.

"With the office closed, you'll have to answer it in the kitchen."

After a few moments, the door to the house opened, and Blake stepped back onto the porch. "That was the secretary for Addie's lawyer Mr. Hassel. He wants you to call and set up an appointment with him."

"Why?"

"She wouldn't tell me. She said his business was with you."

I turned to lock the front door, no longer wanting to get more clothes. "Maybe he wants to tell me that Addie's cousin has inherited the farm and wants me out."

The thought ran through my mind, though, that the lawyer probably wanted to discuss how I would repay the money I owed Addie's estate. I was certainly in no hurry to admit that I was about as broke as I could be.

The crunching of gravel in the driveway caught my attention. I sighed when I recognized Celeste Witherington's SUV pulling to a stop in front of the house. I walked down the steps and waited as she got out and came toward me. Blake followed and stood beside me.

A man I didn't know got out from the driver's side and walked around to stand by Celeste. His black hair gleamed in the sunlight. Sunglasses with silver-coated lenses hid his eyes.

"Oh, chérie," Celeste gushed as she threw her arms around me. "I'm so sorry about Addie. She was such a dear friend." She stepped back, pulled a tissue from her pocket, and dabbed at her eyes. "I still can't believe she's gone."

"Thank you, Celeste." I glanced at Blake and raised an eyebrow.

The man stepped forward, his hand extended. "Miss Dennison, I'm Perry Witherington, Celeste's stepson."

This was certainly a surprise. I'd never heard Addie mention Celeste's stepson.

Perry removed the glasses and slipped them into his shirt pocket. His dark eyes held me captive, casting some kind of hypnotic spell over me. I couldn't respond.

He smiled and cupped my hand in his. "I've been

living in New York, but I've returned to help Celeste run my father's business. I wanted to come with her to extend my sympathy."

For such a hot day, his skin felt cool to the touch. "Thank you, Mr. Witherington."

Blake moved closer to me and stuck out his hand. "I'm Blake Cameron, Miss Dennison's friend."

Perry turned to Blake. He opened his mouth to speak but stopped as a howl from the kennel drifted across the yard.

Celeste looked in the direction of the kennel, and fresh tears rolled down her face. "What's the matter with those poor babies?"

I sighed and shook my head. "They've been that way ever since Addie's death. They must miss her terribly."

"Oui." She brushed at her eyes again and cleared her throat. "You aren't used to taking care of the dogs. Maybe we can help you out. We'd like to make you an offer."

"What kind of offer?"

Celeste dabbed at her eyes with the tissue. She darted a glance to Perry and back to me. "We'd be happy to buy all of Addie's dogs from you."

Perry Witherington put his arm around Celeste's shoulders, hugged her, and directed a smile at me. "Taking care of a kennel of champion dogs must be very difficult for you. We're prepared to give you top price for them."

I heard what they were saying, but I couldn't respond. His eyes still had me in their spell, and I couldn't pull myself away.

"Miss Dennison, did you hear me?" Perry Wither-ington's voice drifted into my ear.

With a start, I pulled my attention back to the two of them. "Do you have the space for them in your kennel?"

Perry glanced at Celeste and tightened his grip on her. "We'll make room for the dogs of my stepmother's dear friend."

A fresh tear rolled down Celeste's face. "Let us do this in memory of Addie."

"Well, I don't know. . ."

Blake leaned over and whispered in my ear. "Leigh, you can't sell the dogs. They don't belong to you."

Where was my brain? Of course, the dogs weren't mine. I looked up at Perry, the spell now broken, and sighed. "I'm sorry. I'll be glad to pass your name on to Addie's lawyer."

"Please do, Miss Dennison." Perry Witherington reached into his pocket, pulled out a business card, and handed it to me. "Tell him to call me, and we can agree on a price."

"I'll tell him."

Perry leaned closer and smiled. "Good. I hope I see you again soon, Miss Dennison." He took his stepmother's arm and turned her toward the car. "We need to go."

He reached out with his free hand and opened the car door then propelled Celeste into the Escalade. With a slight bow to Blake, Perry walked back around to the driver's side of the SUV. The car roared down the driveway.

Blake let out a soft whistle. "There's something about that guy I didn't like."

I watched the car disappear in the distance. "I don't know. I thought he was kind of charming."

Blake frowned and strode toward his truck. We climbed in and headed for the main road. As we drove down the driveway, I looked back at the house that I had called home for the past eight years. My heart ached at the thought that this might possibly be the last time I would be able to call it that.

I'd only met Addie's cousin from Alabama once when he visited, and he seemed to resent my presence. After he inherited the farm, he wouldn't want me around. I wondered how soon I would have to vacate. Where would I go?

━━

Three days later, I was dusting my Queen Anne table when Marcie came out of the workroom in the back of the shop.

She held out a spray bottle of glass cleaner. "Leigh, is this what you've been looking for all morning?"

I smiled and reached for the container. "Yeah. Where did you find it?"

"In the refrigerator. I opened the door to put my lunch inside, and there sat your missing cleaner."

I scrubbed at an imaginary spot on the tabletop.

"Strange. I wonder how it got there."

Marcie chuckled. "Yeah, me, too."

The telephone rang at that moment. Marcie stood still, her eyebrows raised. "Are you going to answer that?"

I moved to the next piece of furniture. "Can you get it while I finish dusting?"

Marcie crossed her arms. "That may be Addie's lawyer. I've run interference for the past few days. Now it's time for you to face him. Ignoring him won't make the problem go away."

I sighed and walked to the phone, hoping it would quit ringing before I got there. "Dennison's Treasure Chest."

"Miss Dennison?" I didn't recognize the female voice.

"Yes, speaking."

"This is Sherry MacKay, Mr. Hassel's secretary. He wants to know if you could come over to his office."

My pulse quickened. "Now?"

"Yes, he really does need to see you. The sooner the better."

I closed my eyes for a moment. I couldn't put it off any longer. "Okay, then. I'll be right over."

I hung up the phone and stood there wondering how soon Addie's cousin would want me to move my belongings out of the house.

❧

Thirty minutes later, I stood in front of her lawyer's office. WILLIAM T. HASSEL, ATTORNEY AT LAW, the sign over the door read. I took a deep breath before I entered and stepped into the cool interior of the building. I had never been in this office before, and the scene before me almost took away my breath.

The feeling I had upon stepping inside was that of entering a living room. A comfortable couch, flanked by two wingback chairs, faced a fireplace. Family pictures adorned the mantel. A Persian rug covered the floor, and what I thought to be reproduction Tiffany lamps sat on tables on either side of the couch.

A young woman, looking just as perfect as the room, sat at a desk that faced the front of the office. She glanced up from her computer, her red manicured nails resting on the keyboard, and smiled.

All the papers and documents on her desk were stacked in neat piles. A small crystal jar held several pens, and a nameplate in front of her stated, SHERRY MACKAY, PARALEGAL.

"May I help you?" Her attention was directed toward me.

"I'm Leigh Dennison"

"Oh yes. I've just started going to the St. Claire Community Church, and I saw you in the choir."

"I remember seeing you there. You'll have to join our Tuesday night Bible study."

"I think I'd like that." My gaze locked on her nails as Sherry reached for a notepad and jotted down a reminder. She rose from her chair and stepped from behind the desk. "Mr. Hassel's expecting you. Follow me please."

"Excuse me." I reached out to stop her.

She turned. "Yes?"

"Just curious. Where do you get your nails done?"

She held up her hand for me to get a better look. "Mary Ann does them at her beauty salon, Tame Your Mane, on Pine Street. Why?"

My nails, chipped and stained from refinishing furniture, had never looked as good as hers did. I wondered if Blake preferred a woman with long, polished fingernails. "I'd like to get mine done, but I don't suppose I can afford it right now."

Sherry laughed. "If you change your mind, tell Mary Ann that I sent you."

She led me to a door at the back of the room, pushed it open, and stepped aside for me to enter. A man rose from his chair behind his desk and came around to greet me.

"Come in, Miss Dennison." He shook my hand and motioned me into a chair facing him. "I'm William Hassel, Mrs. Jordan's lawyer. I don't think we've met, but she told me a lot about you."

Probably how much money I owed her, I thought. My leg started to tremble, and I touched my knee in an effort to keep my foot from tapping out a rhythm on the hardwood floor.

He walked back behind his desk, sat down, and rifled through a stack of papers. "Mrs. Jordan came to me about a year ago to write her will. She knew she wasn't getting any younger and wanted everything taken care of."

My mind whirled. Where in the world could I come up with that amount of money to repay the loan in one lump sum?

Mr. Hassel was talking, but I couldn't focus.

I can hold a big auction and sell all my antiques. Sell my truck if necessary. But that won't even be enough.

"And so, Miss Dennison, it's all yours."

I gave my head a little shake. "What?"

"I said it's all yours."

"I don't understand."

Mr. Hassel leaned forward and clasped his hands in front of him on the desk. "Mrs. Jordan has left her entire estate to you. She wanted you to inherit everything."

My mouth went dry, and I tried to swallow. "But what about her cousin?"

"She left a cash amount for him as she did Ross James."

"She did?"

He pursed his lips. "She asked one thing, though. That you allow Ross to remain employed at the kennel until he completes his education."

I curled my fingers around the arms of my chair and squeezed. "I don't understand. You're telling me that Addie left her estate to me?"

"Yes, with the house, the land, stocks, bank accounts, and all her personal items, you're looking at something in the neighborhood of several million dollars after all the bills are paid."

"M–m–million?"

He stood up, came around his desk, and sat on the corner of it. "I know this has to be a shock to you."

His lips formed the words. I heard what he said, but for some reason it didn't register in my mind. "I plan to probate the will as soon as possible, in fact probably this morning. You can move back into the house anytime. It's yours now." He crossed his arms and smiled at me.

"M–mine?"

He laughed out loud. "Yes. Do you have any questions?"

I still couldn't believe what I'd heard. "You said millions?"

He took off his glasses and twirled them between his fingers. "Maybe you need some time to get used to the idea that you're an heiress." He took me by the arm, helped me rise from the chair, and guided me to the door. "Now don't worry about anything. I'll take care of all the details for you. I'll call you tomorrow to come sign some papers my secretary will have for you."

He ushered me to the door, and the next thing I knew I was standing in the outer office. My gaze drifted across the room and settled on the Tiffany lamps. I stared transfixed at them trying to comprehend what had just happened to me.

"Miss Dennison, are you all right?" Sherry MacKay's red fingernails tapped my arm.

I swallowed before answering. "Just trying to grasp what Mr. Hassel said."

Sherry smiled "I'll let you know when the papers are ready."

"When the papers are ready," I echoed. "Yes. Thanks."

Sherry waved to me as I stepped onto the sidewalk and closed the door. I stood there for several moments before I cracked the door a bit and peered inside. Sherry, back at her desk, looked up and smiled. "Is there something else?"

I swallowed before speaking. "I may get my nails done after all."

With a nod, I closed the door again, straightened my shoulders, and turned to walk back to my antique shop. Addie's face flashed in my mind, and tears pooled in my eyes. I would never know another person who gave love as freely as she did. Even when I owed her so much money, Addie was making arrangements to give me even more.

My reflection in the window of Mr. Hassel's office caught my attention, and I stared at it. "Did he say millions?"

I shook my head, moved to the next store, and stopped. My image greeted me again. I wiped at the tears in my eyes. "I may be an heiress, but I'd give it all up to have Addie back," I whispered.

A honking horn sliced through my thoughts, and I glanced over my shoulder at Blake whose truck sat in the middle of the street. He motioned me toward him. I pulled a tissue from my pocket and dried my tears before I dashed toward the truck and climbed in.

Blake stared at me, a little frown creasing his forehead. "I went by the shop, and Marcie told me you'd walked over to Mr. Hassel's office. I thought I'd pick you up. Is everything all right?"

"I'm fine. Just in a state of shock right now."

His gaze softened, and he reached out and grasped my hand. "Bad news?"

"No, the opposite. I've just found out that Addie left me everything she owned. I've inherited all her estate."

He put the truck in gear and headed down the street. "You're kidding. Are you all right?"

"Not really. I want Addie back, but I know that's not possible."

We rode in silence for a few minutes. The memory of my last conversation with Addie popped into my mind. "The afternoon before Addie was murdered she told me she had something to discuss with me. I didn't know what it was. I wondered why she asked me if I liked. . ." I sat up straight in the seat. "Oh no!"

Blake punched the brakes and the seat belt caught me. "What's the matter?"

Panic gripped me as I turned to look at him. "What am I going to do? All those dogs belong to me now."

Blake let out a long breath. "You scared me. I thought something terrible had happened."

"What am I going to do? I don't know anything about taking care of dogs, and I can't do that and operate my antique shop."

"Well, Celeste wants to buy them."

I remembered Addie asking me if I would make sure her dogs would always be taken care of. Now I understood. She was trying to tell me that she wanted me, not someone else, to provide for them. "I can't sell them."

A car behind us honked, and Blake glanced over his shoulder. "I'm blocking the street. Let's go over to your store, and we'll see if we can't find a solution to your problem."

We drove down the street to the city limits to my shop, parked, and went inside. Every time I walked through the door of Dennison's Treasure Chest, I felt pride at how Marcie and I had remodeled the old building. Thanks to the loan from Addie, it was now stocked with the highest quality antiques in the whole area.

Marcie came out of the workroom when Blake and I entered. She hurried forward. "I've been about to go out of mind wondering what was going on over at that lawyer's office." She covered her mouth with her hand

and then lowered it, her face crimson. "Oh, Leigh, that sounded awful. It's none of my business, but I've just been worried."

I hugged Marcie. "Well, Mr. Hassel told me something that shocked me right out of my mind. As if that's hard to do."

Marcie shook her head in protest. "Don't sell yourself short, girlfriend. As far as I'm concerned, you're the best."

My eyes filled with tears, and I glanced from Marcie to Blake, the two people who now seemed closer to me than anyone else. Marcie listened without speaking while I told her the story.

"But I don't know what I'm going to do about the dogs. I can't take care of them."

Marcie seemed lost in thought. "Maybe there's something you can do," she began. "You said Celeste wants to buy them. Have you thought about selling them to her?"

"Blake mentioned that. But I can't. Addie would want me to take care of them. The more I've thought about it I've decided Celeste and her stepson are the last ones Addie would want to have her dogs."

Surprise flashed across Marcie's face. "I didn't know she had a stepson."

"He runs the business for her now. Maybe I can find someone to help me out for a while."

"I hesitate to suggest this, but how about Ross?" Blake asked. "Why don't you let him come back and take care of them?"

Mr. Hassel's words flashed in my mind. "Addie's will stated that she wanted me to let Ross continue to work there."

"Well, there you have your answer."

I shook my head. "But I still suspect he killed Addie for the money."

"Well, the police haven't arrested him." The tone of Blake's voice held a hint of anger.

I turned to him and glared. "Why are you so quick to defend him?"

Blake relaxed and held up his hands in front of him. "Okay, Leigh. Sorry I mentioned it."

The way he looked at me softened my heart. "I'm sorry. This is just all so new to me."

I sank down on a Louis XV sofa and caressed the velvet upholstery. Blake dropped down beside me, and Marcie sat in the matching chair. We sat in silence for a few moments before Blake turned to me.

"Okay. . .I think I have an idea."

"Do you? What?"

"School doesn't start for over a month. If you'd agree to let Ross come back, I can help out every day. And I can keep an eye on him to make you feel better."

Maybe this was a good idea. I suspected Ross of the murder, but I had to admit I still had some reservations about Blake, too. If I had them together, I could observe them both and find out which one killed Addie.

"Let me think about it."

Marcie cleared her throat as if to get our attention. "Okay, you two. I have a suggestion, too."

I turned to her. "What?"

"I think you need to take some time off from the shop, Leigh. You've been through a lot in the last week, and you've got a lot ahead of you with Addie's estate. Don't worry about the shop. I'll look after it, and when you get everything settled, you can come back to work."

I started to protest, but I stopped. This was perfect. If Ross came back to the kennel, I could keep a watch on both Blake and Ross. I'd observe them just the way my favorite television police officers did when they were watching a suspect.

"Leigh, where are you?" Marcie's voice called to me.

I blinked. "Sorry. My mind strayed for a moment."

Marcie started to speak, but the bell over the door jingled, signaling someone had entered the store. I glanced over my shoulder to see Detective Sawyer making his way toward us.

We stood as he approached. "Good morning, Detective Sawyer," Marcie said.

He smiled at her. "Hello, Miss Payton. It's good to see you again."

A small flush crept across Marcie's cheeks. I stepped between him and Marcie and forced a smile. "Have you come to tell us you've found Addie's killer?" I asked.

Much to my distress, he pulled the notepad from his pocket and sighed. "No, but I do have a few questions,

Miss Dennison, if you have time."

"Certainly."

He glanced around. "Is there somewhere we could talk privately?"

Marcie turned to Blake. "I have some boxes in the storage room that need to be moved. Would you mind helping me?"

Blake hesitated a moment and then followed Marcie toward the back of the store. He glanced at me before he disappeared through the door.

"What can I do for you, Detective Sawyer?" I asked in what I hoped was a cool tone.

He flipped the pad open. "I've just come from the courthouse. One of my friends who works there told me Mrs. Jordan's lawyer just finished probating her will. I understand you've inherited everything."

My mouth felt like I'd stuffed cotton in it. I didn't like the turn of this conversation. "That's correct."

He wrote something down, tilted his head to one side, and glanced around the shop. "And Ross said Mrs. Jordan loaned you the money to start your business. That right?"

My vocal chords refused to work. My eyes grew wider by the moment.

Without waiting for a reply, he leaned closer. "Have you paid back all the money?"

"No." My answer was barely above a whisper.

He scribbled something else in his pad. "And now you won't have to, will you?"

My face felt as if it was on fire. "I don't suppose I will."

"I thought I'd stop by and warn you again not to leave town. Especially with all your newfound wealth."

A retort sprang to my lips, but I thought of Addie. This man had no idea of the agony I'd endured since finding her body. In my grief the night of the murder, maybe I'd alienated him. But in my heart, I knew we both wanted the same thing—to catch a killer. I sighed and tried to smile. "Detective Sawyer, maybe we got off on the wrong foot the other night. I'm just as eager for Addie's killer to be caught as you are. You can be assured I'll be right here until that happens. Is that a 10/7?"

Detective Sawyer frowned. "Uh, you mean am I out of service?"

"No. I meant was my message received?"

"Ah, the armchair detective's at it again. That's a 10/4, Miss Dennison. I understand completely."

He tried to repress a smile as he turned and walked to the door.

Marcie and Blake hurried back into the room as soon as he'd left the shop.

"Oh, Leigh, we were listening from the back," Marcie said. "Are you all right?"

I grasped Marcie's hand. "I'm fine, but did you see how he smiled at you? I think he was actually flirting with you."

Marcie's cheeks flushed. "Well, he is kinda cute."

"Cute?" How could Marcie believe a man who suspected me of murder was attractive? I squeezed her hand tighter. "You really think so?"

Before she could answer, Blake spoke up. "Leigh,

you were wonderful, even if you don't know the police codes."

"Yeah, that wasn't very good, was it? Another example of my mouth taking over before my brain had time to think." The thought of how I'd embarrassed myself made my cheeks hot. "But you two are the wonderful ones. I'm blessed to have two great friends like you. Thanks for offering to help with the shop and the kennel. I'm going to accept your help in both places, because I think I'm going to be very busy for a while."

Blake frowned. "Doing what?"

I took a deep breath. "I'm going to find out who killed Addie."

Marcie's eyes grew wide. "Oh, Leigh, you can't be serious."

Frustration at the events of the past week overcame me. "I am. The police may not like it, but I'm going to find the murderer."

"But you don't know anything about detective work."

"Maybe not, but I have something in my favor that the police don't."

Blake put his hand on my shoulder and turned me to face him. "What?"

Tears stung my eyes. "I loved Addie like a mother, and I'm not going to let her killer go unpunished."

Marcie touched my arm. "Leigh, you know you have a problem staying focused on anything. Remember the glass cleaner in the refrigerator this morning?"

"I know, but I'm going to approach it just like I

do when I build furniture. I'll gather all the pieces and then put them together in one finished product."

Marcie crossed her arms and raised her eyebrows.

"I can do this, Marcie. And I'm going to do it for Addie."

"Leigh." Blake's voice caught my attention. "You don't have to do this alone. I've never tried my hand at anything like this. But I'll do anything you want me to if it'll help us find out who killed Addie."

"Me, too," Marcie said.

Blake and Marcie both put their arms around me, and we stood locked in an embrace. I whispered a prayer of thanks for two such good friends. At least I hoped they were *both* good friends.

Please, God, don't let the murderer be Blake.

After a few moments, Blake pulled away. "Okay. Now how can we help you?"

I remembered the legal pad next to the cash register. Within moments, I was back with it and sat on the sofa.

"First, I'm going to make a list of suspects."

Blake sat down. "Good. You need to get organized. Maybe Marcie and I can help with that."

Organization—that's what I needed. It was time to focus as I'd never been able to do in my life.

For the next half hour we brainstormed back and forth recalling everything that happened the day Addie died. When we seemed to have related every event, I looked at Marcie. "The way I see it, we have two chief suspects—Ross James and Preacher Cochran."

Marcie raised an eyebrow, a smile tugging at her mouth. "That is if we leave you off the list, Leigh." She reached over and patted my knee. "Just kidding."

Blake rubbed his chin, the muscle in his jaw twitching. "I think Preacher Cochran is the likeliest suspect. Leigh saw him holding the murder weapon earlier, and he appears to be an unstable person."

I tapped my pencil against the pad as I pondered Blake's logic. "And he probably needs money. How does someone live if they just wander across the country with no evident income? I knew he was trouble when he moved in under that bridge earlier in the summer. I tried to warn Addie, but she felt sorry for him."

"I hope her kindness didn't backfire on her and cause her to lose her life." Marcie pushed a strand of hair behind her ear and leaned back into her chair. "But what about Ross James?"

Blake frowned and turned to her. "I can't believe Ross had anything to do with this. He's a good kid— just mixed up at the moment."

This was getting us nowhere. We couldn't even agree on who were the most obvious suspects. I held up my hand to signal their attention. "Okay, guys. I think this is what we should do. We have a list of suspects. I think I need to question each of them and see if I can find anything suspicious in their stories."

"Good idea," Blake said. "But you're not going alone. I'll go with you to visit Ross and Preacher. If you find the killer, it could dangerous."

Worried for me! Blake was worried about me. He

wanted to go with me, which meant we would be spending more time together. I also realized I would have more opportunities to observe him for suspicious behavior. My heart told me he couldn't possibly be the killer, but my head didn't agree. I had to find something that would delete him from my list of suspects.

"Thanks, Blake. That's great. Why don't we start tomorrow after we get through at the kennel? We can begin by visiting Preacher Cochran."

"That suits me fine."

"Wait," Marcie said, "I think we're forgetting one more suspect here."

"Who?" Blake and I spoke at the same time.

"Celeste Witherington. Celeste was at the farm that day."

Blake snapped his fingers. "Yeah, and don't forget her strange stepson."

I directed my attention to the legal pad as I jotted down Celeste's name. "Her stepson's not strange. He's a very attractive man."

Blake jumped up. "If you say so." He glanced at his watch. "Well, I think I'd better get busy. I checked on the dogs this morning, but they may need more water. I'm going to run out to the farm."

Marcie glanced from Blake to me. "If you want to go, Leigh, I can hold down the fort here for as long as it takes."

"Thanks, Marcie. I'm going to your house to pick up all my things. It's time I went home and got busy finding out who killed Addie."

Blake strode toward the door, and I trailed behind him. Once outside, he turned to me. "Do you need me to help you get your things at Marcie's?"

"No, I can do it. I'll come home in a little while."

"See you there." He got into his truck, and I watched him drive out of the parking lot.

I headed toward my own vehicle parked beside the shop. When I climbed inside, the heat stole my breath, and I turned the air conditioner up full blast.

I touched the legal pad lying beside me on the seat. The names of Preacher Cochran, Ross James, and Celeste Witherington were written on the first three lines. I touched the fourth. I could not bring myself to write the name of the person I prayed wasn't involved.

As the cool air blew across my face, I wondered if the house would be as hot since the air conditioning had been turned off. I would get my things at Marcie's, and then head home to settle in.

Home—I was going home. But Addie wouldn't be there.

Addie and I had shared a house. We had become a family. And now I was beginning the next part of my life without her. I wondered if it would ever seem the same again. One sure thing echoed through my mind. The identity of Addie's killer couldn't stay hidden long with me on the case.

The engine roared to life as I turned the ignition. "Watch out, whoever you are. Leigh Dennison, armchair detective and avid student of *Law and Order*, is about to bring you down."

6

Two a.m. The red numbers on the digital clock taunted me from the bedside table.

My first night back at home and I was wide-awake. Every nerve in my body tingled in protest.

Maybe I came back too soon.

I had locked every door and window in the house before retiring and even went through the rooms a second time. Now I lay in bed and mentally rechecked each one to make sure I hadn't skipped any.

Added to my insomnia was the problem with the dogs. The howl from the direction of the kennel had gone on for hours.

At one o'clock, I had started to go down to the kennel to see if I could calm them. But then I lay back on my pillow. A killer was still out there somewhere, maybe lurking to strike again. What if he was irritating the dogs in an attempt to lure me from the house? I might be spacey at times, but I had never been accused of being stupid. Those dogs would just have to wait until daylight. With the security system set, I'd be safe inside.

I wish it had been on the night Addie was murdered.

At two thirty, I swung my legs over the side of my bed, slipped into my robe, and headed downstairs to the kitchen. "I wonder if there's anything in the house to eat."

To my relief, when I opened the coffee canister,

the savory aroma of ground, roasted Colombian beans drifted upward. "Nothing better than mountain grown. I wonder if there's bread for toast."

Within minutes, I sat on the couch in the den with my early morning snack. Juggling the cup and saucer, I turned on the television and settled back. The hot coffee warmed me, and I munched on the toast as I flipped through the channels. A rerun of the Eukanuba Dog Show flashed onto the screen just as another howl arose from the kennel. With a groan I clicked the remote, fast forwarding until a Lifetime for Women movie appeared.

After a few minutes, I snuggled down on the sofa, stretched out, and yawned. The next thing I knew loud knocking jerked me from a sound sleep. Sunlight poured through the den windows, and to my surprise, the clock on the wall pointed to eight o'clock. I jumped up, still half asleep, my knee jarring the coffee table. My half-filled cup tilted before turning over and spilling the remains of my coffee.

The brown liquid flowed across the surface toward the edge of the table. My first impulse was to stop the spreading stream with the only thing available—my robe. I jerked it from around my body, wadded it into a ball, and sopped up the spill.

"I'm coming," I yelled, hoping whoever was at the door heard me.

I slipped my arms into the sleeves of the robe, and I tied the sash around my waist. "What a mess!" I touched the large smear across the top of the housecoat.

A dark stain stood out on the white terry cloth. I rubbed my hand over the huge, damp spot that seeped through to my skin. My attention was now focused on the robe, not on answering the door. "How can I answer the door looking like this?"

The knock sounded again.

I glanced around the room for the matching scuffs, but they were nowhere to be found. Clutching the wet robe around me, I headed toward the door barefooted, but my little toe caught on the corner of the couch. "Ow! Ouch! Oh my!" I cried, hopping across the floor on one foot.

The pain increased as I hobbled toward the door. In the hallway mirror, my eyes caught a glimpse of my reflection, a most horrible sight. My hair stood up on my head like my finger had just encountered an electrical outlet.

"Whoever this is better have a good reason for coming by so early in the morning."

I reached the door and jerked it open and then wished I was anywhere else but standing there facing Blake Cameron. His hair, a little damp and curling on his forehead, looked as if he had just stepped out of the shower. And he smelled good, too.

"Good morning, Leigh. Did you sleep well on your first night back?"

How could anybody look like that and act so happy this early in the morning? My mind didn't kick in until I'd had my second cup of coffee. I searched my fuzzy mind for a snappy retort, but my brain seemed to be still asleep. I sagged against the door. "Blake, I didn't expect you this early."

"I came to take care of the dogs, and then we're going to visit Preacher Cochran. Did you forget?"

I was beginning to gather my wits, and an awful thought hit me. Blake Cameron had seen me in a coffee-stained robe, barefooted, and hair that resembled a porcupine.

"I haven't forgotten. I'm just not ready."

A smile pulled at his lips as his gaze traveled over me. "Why don't I go feed the dogs while you get dressed? I'll come back when I get through."

"Fine." I pushed on the door, wanting it closed.

The door met an obstacle, his hand pushing from the other side. "Why don't you fix us some coffee? That is if you have any left after spilling it all."

I wrapped my robe tightly around my body and straightened to my full height. "I'll have you know I've had an awful night. And then you show up before I even have a chance to make myself presentable."

He grinned. "You look good to me."

Before I had a chance to respond, he hopped off the porch and headed toward the kennel, leaving me to wonder if he was serious or just teasing me.

———

Fresh from the shower and dressed for the day, I felt a tingle of happiness as I set the table on the screened-in back porch for Blake and me. On mornings like this with the sun shining and the cool mountain air stirring the leaves on the trees, I couldn't imagine a more beautiful place on earth. Being outside was always a joy for me, but I had to admit there was an ulterior motive to my actions this morning. Blake was still on my list of suspects, and I didn't want to be alone inside with a suspected murderer.

The back door banged, and Blake stepped onto the porch. He looked at the table, smiled, and held up his hands. "Mind if I go inside to wash up?"

"Sure. There's a sink just inside the door in the laundry room."

He disappeared inside and was back in a few minutes.

"This looks good, Leigh," he said as he took his seat. He reached for his napkin and spread it across his lap. "I'm glad you set the table outside."

My heart thumped. Did he know I suspected him? "Why?"

He swallowed and then looked into my eyes. "We've got a great friendship developing here, and I don't want to do anything to compromise it. Keep everything out in the open, so to speak. Do you understand?"

Relief washed through me. "Yes."

"Good." He smiled. "Now let me bless this food, and we'll eat."

While Blake prayed, my conscience hurt as if I'd betrayed the nicest guy in the world by doubting him. How could I have ever thought Blake could hurt anyone?

—

Later, after we'd finished, we discussed our agenda for the day. Since Preacher Cochran lived nearby and was a chief suspect, we decided to visit him first.

"I never liked him hanging around here, but Addie felt sorry for him."

Blake swallowed a mouthful of food before responding. "What do you know about him?"

"Nothing except he's a Vietnam veteran."

"Where did he get the nickname *Preacher*?"

A vague memory stirred of something Addie told me. "Seems like he was involved in something bad." I thought for a moment, trying to remember what Addie had said, but nothing came to me. I shrugged. "Whatever it was, he lectured everybody he came in contact with afterwards about repenting of past wrong deeds. His friends started calling him Preacher, and it stuck."

"Something that happened in Vietnam, you think?"

"Maybe. Addie offered to let him stay in the room over my workshop, but he wouldn't do it. Said he liked the outdoors. From what Addie said, he's been wandering across the country for years. She said he never readjusted to life in the States after Vietnam."

"I've read where that happened to a lot of people. I can understand why Addie felt concern for him."

"Come on, Blake. Don't you go feeling sorry for our suspects before we even talk to them. You have to keep an unbiased opinion."

He set down the cup he had just picked up and stared at it for a moment before he replied. "Can you do that, Leigh?"

"Can I do what?"

"Keep an unbiased opinion. Don't jump to any conclusions too quickly. Your TV detectives don't."

My face warmed under his stare. "Well, I have to admit I never liked Preacher or Ross. And now I don't trust them."

He propped his elbows on the table and leaned forward, a somber expression on his face. "Just remember that Addie trusted them. From what I knew about her, she always treated people the way she thought Jesus would. Can we do any differently?"

I stood and began to stack the dishes. "Well, we're wasting time sitting here talking. Let's get on with our visit to Preacher."

Blake stood beside me, stuck his hands in his pockets, and took a deep breath. "Sorry, if I've offended you, but. . ."

At that moment, a howl arose from the direction of the kennel. Blake glanced away. "What's the matter now? They were fine when I left them. I'll go check and be right back."

I took the dishes inside as Blake walked back to the kennel and then went out the front door toward his truck parked in the circle drive in front. As I reached for the car door handle, a loud growl rumbled from the front seat. Before I could react, the head of the biggest bloodhound I'd ever seen in my life appeared in the open window. His wet nose pressed against my cheek, and his long tongue licked at my face.

"Aargh!" I jumped backwards and tumbled to the ground.

Blake rounded the corner of the house just at that moment and rushed to my side. "What's the matter?"

I pointed at the truck. "That dog. It tried to bite my face!"

He laughed and pulled the door open. "Bad boy, Red. You've scared Leigh to death. Now aren't you ashamed of yourself? Come on outta there."

A scratching sound came from the seat, and then a dog that must have weighed at least one hundred pounds lumbered out. The skin around his face hung in deep folds. He looked up at Blake with a solemn expression. Blake reached down and scratched the bloodhound behind his ears.

This had to be the one Addie had told me about. "Is—is this your dog?"

Blake knelt down next to him and looped his arm around the massive neck. "Leigh, I want you to meet Red. He was just trying to get acquainted." There was no mistaking the affection in his voice.

The dog looked at me and then at Blake. His powerful jaws moved, not in a menacing way but almost in an affectionate manner. His tail, which curved upward and over his back, seemed to give an essence of nobility to his stance. I stepped a little closer, bent down, and touched the top of the dog's head. "Hello, Red."

Red inched closer to me, his tongue directed toward my arm. Blake stood up. "He likes you."

"Well, he gave me quite a scare. I wasn't expecting to be licked to death."

"Sorry. I forgot to tell you he came along with me this morning." Blake went around to the back of the truck, Red at his heels, and let the tailgate down.

As if on signal, the dog jumped into the back of the truck. I climbed into the vehicle as Blake shut the end gate and jumped in next to me. "What was the matter with the dogs?"

Blake shrugged. "I don't know. They stopped howling when they saw me." He turned the ignition. "Ready?" he asked, and we roared off down the driveway.

From time to time, I glanced through the window behind me as we rode along. Red lay in the back of the truck, his eyes closed.

What a change had taken place in my life. Addie was gone. Every time I looked around I expected to see her, but I knew she wasn't coming back. And I'd never been a dog lover, but now I found myself the owner of a kennel of champion show dogs and the traveling companion of a big, red bloodhound. Life can be very unpredictable.

We drove along the road beside the meandering river until we came to the bridge nearest the farm. Blake turned off the highway and guided the truck down the path that fishermen in the area used to get to the stream. He stopped at the river's edge.

Preacher stood on the bank, a fishing pole in his

hand. He looked around as we approached, pulled his line from the water, and wrapped it around the rod he held.

I poked Blake in the ribs with my elbow. "Pretty fancy fishing gear. I wonder where he got the money to buy it."

Blake guided me forward. "Maybe we can find out."

My gaze traveled toward the bridge several hundred yards upstream and over the area Preacher occupied. His belongings, stacked in the darkness under the concrete supports, stirred my interest, but it was impossible to identify anything at this distance.

"Can I help you?" Preacher asked, a sullen expression lining his face.

Blake stuck out his hand. "I'm Blake Cameron. I think you know Miss Dennison. We want to talk to you about Mrs. Jordan."

"The police done been here and talked to me. I told them everything I know."

I narrowed my eyes and stared at him. "Did you tell them how I found you holding the weapon that was later used to kill Addie?"

"Yeah, I told them how I went in your shop and how you run me out."

I stepped closer to Blake. "Why were you looking at the mortise chisel?"

Preacher shrugged. "No reason. I'd just finished helping Miss Addie clean out the kennel, and I was on my way back to my bridge when I noticed the door open. I saw her talkin' to her friend, that highfalutin lady in the big car, and I thought they wouldn't notice if I just took a look inside."

Blake stepped a little closer to him. "Mr. Cochran, how did you get along with Mrs. Jordan?"

To my surprise tears formed in Preacher's eyes. "She's the first person in years who's treated me with any kindness. I never met nobody like her. She was an angel. Yes, sir, an angel." He turned his face away from us, his hands hanging to his side, and gazed across the river. "I woulda died in her place if I'd had the chance."

With a groan, Preacher dropped the fishing rod to the ground and sank down next to it. He rocked back and forth on the riverbank as if in agony.

Blake glanced at me, and we sat down on each side of him. When he gained control of himself, Blake reached out and touched Preacher's shoulder. "What brought you to St. Claire and to this bridge?"

"I don't talk about it much. But I told Miss Addie."

"But maybe something you told her would help us find her killer. You want us to do that, don't you?"

He swiped his face with his shirt sleeve. "Yeah."

I scooted closer to him. "Then tell us what you told Addie. It may not help, but then again it might."

Preacher bit his lip. He let out a long breath and stared into space for several minutes before he began to speak. "It was Vietnam, you know. She wanted to help me 'cause her son died there." He hesitated for a moment, his body still rocking. "Sometimes I wish I hadn't come back either. Too many memories."

"What happened to you there?" I asked.

Preacher wrapped his arms around his knees. "Bad times."

He sat silent with his eyes closed for a few moments before he began again. "I was nineteen years old and just out of high school when I joined the Army and was sent to Vietnam. My company was a sorry bunch of misfits." His eyes held a glazed look, and he paused for a moment. "We thought we was tough, but we was just scared kids ready for some action when we moved into Quang Ngai Province. It was full of Viet Cong, and you couldn't trust nobody. The military burned nearly all the homes in the area, and homeless people was everywhere. Every day you heard about soldiers poisoning wells or some young girl gettin' raped. We even got rewarded for kills so the officers could report big body counts to the top brass in Saigon."

Blake gave a little whistle. "I've heard lots of stories about Vietnam, but I never knew that."

Preacher stared into the distance. "Yeah, it happened. The GIs had a saying—anything that was dead and wasn't white was a Viet Cong."

"How awful," I said.

He gave a humorless laugh. "Oh, that wasn't nothing to what would happen later. In the spring of my first year there, we got orders to go to a little village, one that was suspected of aiding the Viet Cong. I heard the women and children was to be evacuated before we burned the town, but it didn't turn out that way."

"I know this story. It was My Lai, wasn't it?" Blake asked.

Preacher turned tortured eyes to Blake. "Not My Lai but another situation too similar. We went into that village, and everybody just went crazy. We started pullin' the people out of their houses and questionin' them. Then the shootin' started. I saw things that day I still can't forget—women and children shot, people forced into a drainage ditch and mowed down with gunfire, some women kneelin' outside a temple shot in the back of the head."

"How terrible," I murmured.

Tears rolled down his face. "Yeah, it's a good thing all the GIs weren't like us. Most of the guys tried to help the people while they were there. But not us. Not us."

I leaned forward and touched his arm. "What about you? Did you shoot anyone?"

He shook his head from side to side. "I don't think so. It's hard to remember all that happened that day. I remember being behind a house on my knees prayin' for it to be over. I put my hands over my ears to block out the screams. It seemed like it went on for hours. When it was all over, there was about five hundred people dead. I still hear those screams in my mind every day."

Blake looked at me. "I've read the accounts of massacres like that. The military tried to cover them up, but only one person ever stood trial. He was paroled by the Secretary of the Army."

"Yeah," Preacher said, "and I asked for a transfer outta there. They sent me to a camp outside Saigon. They'd sprayed the land around it with Agent Orange to kill the foliage so the enemy couldn't hide in it." He snorted a little laugh. "It kept the Viet Cong out all right, but we didn't know we was breathin' somethin' that would be our biggest enemy. I guess my exposure to it was a punishment for what I done."

The story he told touched me. But there was still the matter of Addie's death. "I understand now why Addie wanted to help you, but I still want to find out why someone would murder her. What can you say to make us believe you had nothing to do with it?"

He turned his head and stared into my eyes. "I couldn't face my family when I came home. I left, and I haven't been back. Miss Addie knew what drove me to wander across the country, and she tried to help me. Like I said, she was an angel. I didn't want her money, and I didn't kill her!"

The tone of his words chilled me, but I knew I had to find out more. "How do you get money to live on?"

"I do odd jobs wherever I go. It don't take much for me. I live off the land as best I can. When I need money, I wash dishes in a restaurant or anything else I can find. Miss Addie paid me to help her take care of her dogs. I sure do like them little fellas."

"They're something else, all right," I said as I got up and brushed at my slacks. "We won't detain you from your fishing any longer."

Blake got up and stuck out his hand. "Thanks for talking with us, Mr. Cochran. We'll be seeing you around."

Preacher ignored the gesture, picked up his fishing

rod, and adjusted the line. "Yeah. See you around."

Without another word, we left him standing on the bank. Back at the truck, Red stuck his nose over the side of the truck bed and licked at my arm. I patted the dog's head. "Good boy."

I hopped up in the seat and glanced over at Blake. His hand was on the ignition key, but he sat there staring at me, a half smile on his face. "What is it?" I asked.

He turned the ignition. "Nothing. I'm just glad you like Red."

We drove in silence back toward the farm. As we turned in the driveway, my curiosity got the better of me. "What did you think?"

Blake sighed. "I just don't know. He has quite a story."

"Yeah, and a violent past."

Blake drove past the house and down to the kennel. "Leigh, promise me you won't go alone to see Preacher until the murderer is caught."

"I don't see why I'd need to." I reached for the door handle.

He turned and placed his hands on my shoulders, halting my exit from the truck. "I'm serious. I want you to promise me." His eyes held a look of fear.

"Why are you so insistent?"

His fingers tightened on my arm, and he swallowed. "I have this sick feeling in the pit of my stomach that we may have just scratched the surface with Preacher Cochran."

The next morning I bounded out of bed the minute the alarm sounded. Blake Cameron would not find me unprepared for the day again. Dressed and eager for his arrival, I buzzed about the kitchen, waiting for the water to drip through the coffeepot. "I'll be sitting in the front porch swing, sipping my first cup of the day when he arrives."

I could envision how I would look. I'd rise gracefully, toss my long hair over my shoulder, and invite him to join me for a breakfast fit for a king. "You shouldn't have gone to so much trouble for me," he would say. And I would assure him it was no bother, just the same as I cooked each morning.

And then he would. . .I stared at the hot water I had just poured into my cup. "Oh no," I groaned. "I forgot to put the coffee in the pot."

I glanced at my watch. Blake would arrive any minute. I grabbed the coffee canister, but it slipped from my hands and crashed to the floor, scattering the contents across the tile.

A loud honk in the driveway caught my attention, and I froze. There was no time to clean up the mess now. I dashed for the front of the house and descended the steps just as Blake climbed from the truck. Red rode in the back but jumped out and lumbered over to me.

"Good morning, Red." His tongue lapped at my hand in greeting as I patted his head. Blake frowned. "What do you think you're doing, Red? Trying to make time with my girl?"

My heart jumped. His girl? Did Blake really think of me that way? Nothing would make me happier, *unless* he was a murderer.

Blake rubbed the dog behind the ears and held a sack out to me. "I don't want to show up every morning expecting you to feed me. So I stopped by the bakery and bought some donuts for breakfast. Think you could spare me a cup of coffee after I've taken care of the dogs?"

"Great. Meet me on the back porch when you get through." Surely enough coffee could be recovered to make one pot.

With a smile, he disappeared around the corner of the house before I started up the steps. A bark from the direction of the truck stopped me. Red, his deep-set eyes staring at me, sat on his haunches in the driveway.

I held the front door open and jerked my head toward the inside. "What are you waiting for? Come on in."

The dog lifted his head, barked once, and moved up the steps, his body and the deep folds around his face swinging back and forth. He brushed against my legs but stopped in the entry and waited for me.

I had to admit Red was a beautiful dog. I remembered my last conversation with Addie when she'd told me about Blake's dog.

Maybe it's good that I've made friends with his dog. It gets me closer to Blake.

"This way, boy." I jerked my thumb in the direction of the kitchen. Red's footsteps padded behind me. For some reason Red and I seemed to hit it off from the moment we met, and it felt comfortable to have some companionship in the empty house.

When we entered the kitchen, Red looked around and studied the room. I dropped to my knees and shook my finger in his face. "I'm swearing you to secrecy. You can never tell Blake about the spilled coffee. Understand?"

Red raised his head and barked. With a swish of his tail he ambled across the floor to the sink and settled himself on the throw rug Addie always kept there to guard the floor from splashing water. A small beam of light streamed through the window above the sink, and Red stretched his head upward in it as if to welcome the warmth.

I put my hands on my hips and laughed. "It looks like you've just filed squatter's rights. So, please, make yourself at home."

His head turned, and his dark eyes followed me as I scooped up the coffee from the top of the pile in the floor then swept up the rest. With the pot filled and dripping, I pulled my legal pad from a drawer and looked at what I'd written a few days earlier.

When the coffee finished dripping, I took the pot and a tray with the cups, saucers, and donuts on it to the back porch. Red followed.

I poured myself a cup and settled in one of the chairs, Red at my feet and the legal pad in front of me. "Okay, Red, let's see who our suspects are. So far Preacher Cochran, Ross James, and Celeste Witherington are the obvious choices, even though the police have me on their list." I glanced at the dog. "Well, I do have one more, but I don't think you'd like to hear that."

A growl rumbled in the dog's throat.

I laughed. "Don't tell me you can read my mind. Okay, I won't say anything else about that."

Red's head bobbed up and down, a loud sniff escaping his large nostrils.

Maybe he was thirsty. I jumped up from my chair. "Where are my manners? I haven't even offered you anything to drink. Let me get you some water."

I returned to the kitchen, filled a bowl, and placed it in front of him. "I think I'm going to enjoy entertaining you. At least I'm not talking to myself anymore."

Squatting down next to the gorgeous animal, I rubbed his head. His eyes stared into mine, and then he lowered his head and lapped at the water.

I thought of all the hours Addie had spent with her dogs, and I began to understand the bond that could grow between an individual and a pet. Remorse filled me at how I had ignored the kennel since Addie's death and had not helped Blake with her dogs, or rather *my* dogs.

Was I taking advantage of Blake's good nature? I shook my head. Blake was helping me until the dogs were sold. When they were gone, would he still come around?

"Coffee ready?" Blake's voice called.

"Come on in," I answered.

Blake saw me beside Red and smiled. The dog swiveled his head, glanced at Blake but turned his attention back to the bowl of water.

Blake sat down, poured himself a cup of coffee. "Shall we pray?" After he'd blessed our food, he reached for a donut. "I think everything's covered at the kennel for the time being."

"Thanks. I don't know what I would have done without you these past few days."

He waved his hand in protest and then raised an eyebrow toward Red. "Well, it looks like you've made yourself at home."

"Red and I are becoming buddies."

"Good." He took a sip from his cup. "I've enjoyed the time we've been spending together."

I swallowed before answering. "I have, too."

A loud bark rang out behind me. Blake chuckled. "I think Red's jealous. You seem to have stolen his affection from me."

My brows raised in what I hoped was a provocative expression. "Which goes to show that males are fickle. Their interests lie in making new conquests."

He held my gaze. "Not me, Leigh. I went on to graduate school straight from college. For the past five years, I've been concentrating on my career. I haven't had much time for a relationship with a woman. But

I know God will lead me to the right person. How about you?"

My heart pounded so hard I thought it must be visible through my blouse. "My parents were killed when I was in college. I came back here after I graduated and worked at the Tourist Center downtown for two years before I opened my shop a year ago."

He smiled. "Well, here I am pushing thirty, and you're not far behind. Maybe the best is about to come for us."

What could I say? I wanted to believe that Blake might come to care for me, but I couldn't open myself up to the possibility of getting my heart broken. Especially if he was a killer. I sat in thought for a moment and then did what always worked when trying to avoid an uncomfortable situation—changed the subject.

"Right now I want to find Addie's killer. Are you ready to question Ross James today?"

A little flash of sorrow glimmered in Blake's eyes before he picked up his cup and took a drink. "Sure. I'm ready anytime you are."

We finished our breakfast in silence; then I stood up. "Ready to go, boy?" The dog jumped up to follow me toward the front of the house.

Blake brought up the rear and didn't say a word until we got to the truck. He let the tailgate down, and Red jumped into the back and settled down. Once inside Blake turned a somber face toward me.

"I want you to go easy on Ross. He's had a rough time, and I don't want to see him hurt anymore than he's already been."

I sighed and gripped the legal pad in my lap. "I'll try to be civil. But he still seems the logical suspect."

Blake grunted, started the truck, and drove down the driveway. When we passed the bridge on the winding road into town, I strained to catch a glimpse of Preacher, but he was nowhere in sight. Where did he go, and what did he do all day?

Twenty minutes later Blake stopped the truck at a small house on the outskirts of town. Even though the houses on the street looked run-down, this home appeared freshly painted with neat flowerbeds across the front. An old truck sat in the driveway, its hood up. Tools lay on the front fender.

Blake pointed toward the vehicle. "Ross has been working on this truck for some time now. He's just about to get it running."

"How do you know that?"

"I told you he was one of my students. I've tried to keep up with what's going on in his life."

We stepped onto the front porch, and Blake knocked. Someone moved around inside and then the door opened. Ross's eyes narrowed when he saw me, and his mouth drew into a grim line.

"What do you want?"

"Good morning, Ross," Blake said. "We wanted to talk to you for a minute. Do you mind if we come in?"

He looked from me to Blake and hesitated before he pushed the door open. "Sure, come on in Mr. Cameron."

He turned, and we followed him into the living room of the house. The small room had little furniture, but everything seemed neat and orderly. *His mother must be a good housekeeper*, I thought, as my gaze moved over the polished end tables and the spotless floor. Not a speck of dust in the whole place. We sat down on a small couch, and Ross sat across from us.

"What do you want to talk to me about?"

Blake scooted to the edge of the couch. "Leigh's trying to find out what happened the day Addie was killed, and she wants to go over your account one more time."

"I've already told—" he began.

"Ross." A low-pitched voice drifted into the room from the back of the house.

A look of apprehension crossed his face, and he jumped up from where he sat. "I'll be right back."

Blake and I looked at each other. I shrugged, opened the legal pad, and began to read over the notes I had made about what Ross had told us about why he left town. The sound of a faucet being turned on and more footsteps came from the other room.

After about five minutes, Ross appeared in the room again and sat. He slumped in his chair and rubbed his hand over his eyes.

"Ross, what's the matter?" Blake leaned forward, his elbows propped on his knees.

Ross looked up and blinked, but I was certain I

saw tears in his eyes. "That was my mother," he said. "She had a treatment yesterday afternoon, and she had a bad night. I thought she'd gone to sleep, but she needed some of her medicine."

"What's the matter with her?" I asked.

He wiped at his eyes before he answered. "She has cancer. . .lymphoma is what the doctor calls it. We're about halfway through the chemo treatments, and we're starting radiation next week, too. I don't know if she's strong enough to do both, but the doctor says we have to do this."

I glanced toward the other room and back at him. "I'm sorry, Ross. I didn't know about your mother."

He looked up, and I caught my breath at the tortured look in his eyes. "You didn't? Miss Addie knew. I thought she probably told you."

"No, she never said a word." Why didn't she tell me? I thought we talked about everything. Could it have been because she thought I wouldn't have cared?

Ross let out a long breath. "Yeah, Miss Addie did everything she could to help us. She drove my mother to her treatments and stayed a lot of days with her until I got through at the kennels. She gave me extra money when she knew we were running short."

I leaned back into the couch cushions and crossed my arms. "Really?"

His face hardened. "I know what you're thinking. But I didn't kill her. There's not enough money in the world that would have made me raise a hand against that woman."

Blake sat still but spoke up. "Ross, why did you argue with Addie the day she was killed?"

Ross raked his hand through his hair and looked at Blake. "I've nearly gone crazy remembering how I talked to her that day. After all she'd done for me, I yelled awful things at her. I don't think I'll ever forgive myself for that." He gave a little laugh and shook his head. "I guess all the kids at school were right. I'm just a no-good Indian after all."

Neither Blake nor I spoke but gave him time to compose himself. When he had, he began again. "My mother's a good woman, but she's had a hard life. She married my father when she was just a young girl. She didn't know how mean he could be when he was drinking. He made our lives miserable for as long as I can remember. The night he got drunk and ran off the road over at Black Mountain, I thought maybe we'd finally have some peace."

He got up, walked to the window, and stared outside. "Yeah, I don't mind telling you I was glad when he died. Mrs. Jordan said that was wrong to feel that way, but I thought now my mother's free."

He glanced over his shoulder at us. "She's a descendant of John Ross, you know. He was a great Cherokee chief. Led our people on the march out of the Smokies and to Oklahoma on the Trail of Tears." He paused for a moment, and the silence hovered in the room. "*Nunna-da-ul-tsun-yi*," he whispered. "Trail where they cried."

Blake leaned forward, his elbows on his knees.

"How long has your mother been sick?"

Ross took a deep breath, straightened his shoulders, and stuck his hands in his pocket. "We found out the month after my father's death. She didn't even have time to enjoy her freedom."

"Why did you drop out of school?" Blake asked.

"I had to take care of her. There wasn't anybody else, and Miss Addie gave me the job so I could do it."

"I don't understand," I interrupted. "If you thought so much of Addie, why were you yelling at her that day in her study?"

The muscle in Ross's jaw twitched. "Miss Addie had been talking to me about getting my GED. She said I couldn't do anything if I didn't have that high school diploma. She told me my people suffered in the past and survived it, and I had to be an example for the next generation. I got mad and told her to quit meddling in my business."

"I heard you say that," I said.

"But I went back later and told her I was sorry for talking to her like that. She said I'd never been over to Cherokee to find out about my ancestors, and I needed to learn from them. She gave me money." He glanced at me, the corners of his mouth drawn down. "And it wasn't from that missing bank deposit. She handed me the keys to her truck and said she'd check on my mother while I was gone."

"So is that what you did?" Blake asked.

Ross looked at Blake. "I'm telling the truth, Mr. Cameron. I went to Cherokee. I visited Oconaluftee Village to find out the history of my people. I even went to see that outdoor drama they put on in the summer."

"*Unto These Hills?*"

"Yeah. I didn't know the story about how the Cherokee were driven out of this part of the country. And I talked with the people. *My people.* I found out I have a great heritage. John Ross dedicated his life to trying to make life better for the Cherokee. I can't waste what he wanted to give our people. I came home to tell Miss Addie she was right. I was going back to school to get my GED, but she wasn't there."

The story Ross told touched me, but I still wasn't convinced he was innocent. He'd told a good story, but that just might be all it was—a story. And he admitted he needed extra money because of his mother's illness.

I started to push to my feet, but a thought popped into my mind. What was it Addie had said to me? *You don't need to try to preserve the past when there are so many people in the present who need help.*

I glanced toward the door that led to the back of the house, and sorrow pricked my heart for the woman in the bedroom. "Ross, I'd like to help get your mother to her appointments."

A look of surprise flashed across his face. "You would?"

"Yes. Let me know what her schedule is. I'll be glad to drive her, and I'm sure some of the people in my Bible study group will, too."

"That would be great, Miss Dennison."

Blake smiled at me. "I'll help, too, Ross."

Ross turned his head away and wiped at his eyes. "I appreciate that."

I stood up and smoothed my hands over my slacks. "Blake, we need to go. I'm sure Ross has other things to do."

Ross led us toward the door. "How's the little fellow doing?" he asked.

I frowned. "Who?"

"The puppy."

"Oh," I said, "you mean Macris Labelle?"

Ross gave a little laugh. "Well, that's not what we called him. Purebred dogs have to have a fancy registered name like he has—Macris Labelle Beaumont III. But they have a call name that they answer to, and we named him Astro. You know, short for Asteroid."

"Asteroid?" Then I remembered. Astro was the nickname Addie used.

He laughed and stood still for a moment as if in thought. "Yeah. Miss Addie told me one time that the chances of a dog like Astro being born with such perfection to its standard were about as great as an asteroid hitting the earth. She said if one did collide with us, the impact would be just as catastrophic as what Astro is going to do to the competition in the show ring. There's not gonna be a dog that can touch him."

"You really think he's that good?" Blake asked.

"Oh, yeah," Ross said. "Miss Addie's been teaching me how to train her terriers, and she's taught me how they're judged." His voice caught in his throat. "She said I was the one who would have him in the ring at

Westminster when he wins Best in Show. I sure hope the little fellow gets his chance."

Blake and I walked back toward his truck. As he opened the door, he smiled at me. "That was a very nice thing you did in there."

I climbed in the truck. "Thanks, but Ross's comments about Addie's hopes for the puppy disturb me."

"Why?"

"I'll never be able to get Astro ready for the show ring."

"Then maybe you'd better sell the dogs."

I hadn't told Blake about my conversation with Addie the day she died, but I remembered her words. I shook my head and adjusted my seat belt. "I can't."

As we drove home, I tried to find a solution, but I couldn't think of any.

8

Blake and I were silent all the way back to the farm. Our visit with Ross had given me much to think about.

The sun reflected off the sign over the farm's entrance as we drove in. I read the words as I did each time I came home and wondered how I could ever live up to the confidence Addie must have had in me to leave me her treasured possessions.

Blake glanced in the rearview mirror. "I think you've got company."

I turned around to glance behind us. "Oh no."

"What?"

"It's Celeste Witherington's car."

Blake pulled to a stop in front of the house, and I got out prepared to meet Celeste. To my surprise Perry Witherington and an elderly man climbed out of the SUV. Perry walked toward me, his silver sunglasses gleaming in the sunlight.

Perry flashed his wide-mouthed smile at me and pulled off his glasses. "It seems we arrived at just the right time." He pointed to the man with him. "This is George Daniels. He's worked for our family ever since I can remember. George, this is Leigh Dennison and her friend."

George smiled at me. "Nice to meet you, Miss Dennison."

"I'm glad to meet you, too."

George covered my hand with both of his. "I'm so sorry about Miss Addie. She was a fine lady." The sympathy I saw in his face warmed me.

"Thank you, Mr. Daniels. Did you know her well?"

He shook his head. "Not well, but I talked with her when she would visit Celeste's kennel. I often told Celeste that in all my years I worked with Mr. Perry's father I never met a more knowledgeable breeder than Miss Addie."

"What a nice compliment." Although Celeste and Perry had offered their condolences, theirs hadn't had the ring of sincerity like George's words.

"Did you ever come to Addie's kennel to see her dogs?"

"No, this is my first time here. I'm sorry I never got a chance to see her work." The man glanced at Perry. "I'll just wait in the car until you finish your business, Mr. Perry."

Perry glanced at George. "Okay."

George turned and walked back to the car just as loud howls rose from the direction of the kennel. Blake's brows pulled together in a frown. "There they go again. I'll go check on them." He glanced at Perry and back at me before disappearing in the direction of the kennel.

Perry replaced his sunglasses and followed me up the stairs to the porch and toward the swing, but I stopped at the thought that he might sit next to me there. A wicker chair seemed the best choice, and I sank down in it.

"We can't figure out what's wrong with the dogs. They've barked and howled ever since Addie's death."

"They probably miss Mrs. Jordan."

"Perhaps."

Perry moved to the swing, sat down, and in slow motion removed his glasses. "I think you're doing a wonderful job taking care of Addie's animals, but you must admit you're inexperienced. Terriers take such extra special care to grow into the show dogs we want. Only an expert in training dogs can do that."

"I know. Do you have any experience in training dogs?"

"I worked with my father while I was growing up. But I've been gone for years." He glanced toward the SUV. "George is one of the best, though. He and my father had great success in the show ring with the dogs they bred."

"I'm sure George and Celeste are happy to have you back."

Perry settled back, crossed his legs, and rested his arm across the back of the swing. "She needed some help running the business. I felt I owed it to my father to help." Perry gave a little push with his foot, and the swing swayed. "I heard that you inherited Addie's estate, so now you can dispose of her property. Is that correct?"

News traveled fast in our town. "Yes."

Perry reached up and pulled a checkbook from his shirt pocket. "Then maybe we can do some business.

I'll buy the dogs today. That'll relieve you of one thing you have to be concerned about. With your shop and the work to keep this place up, I know you don't really have the time to devote to the dogs."

"How did you know I have a shop?"

"Celeste told me."

Perry whipped a pen out and began to write on the check. With a flourish, he held it out to me. I'd never seen such a string of zeros in my life. "I knew show dogs were expensive, but I didn't know they ranked right up there with the price of gold."

Perry held the check closer, dangling it before me in temptation. "Take it, Leigh. We can finish up this business right now."

I shook my head. "I'm sorry. I can't sell the dogs."

Perry's eyes narrowed, and he held the check even closer to me. "It's best for everybody, Leigh. I know you're trying hard. But your taking care of purebred dogs is like a furniture salesman from a discount house running your antique shop. You have to know what you're doing. Just take this, and all your worries with the dogs will be over."

I drew back a little. Why were Perry and Celeste so determined to buy the dogs? Were they just used to getting their own way, or was I missing something?

I thought of the legal pad and mentally filled in the fourth line with Perry's name. He and Celeste needed to be studied more carefully.

"I'm sorry, Perry. The dogs aren't for sale."

Perry frowned and started to speak, but a loud

bark from Blake's truck stopped him. Red stood in the truck bed, his eyes directed toward the corner of the house. Just then Blake appeared, with Beau and Belle's puppy in his arms.

"All right, little fellow," he cooed. "It's gonna be all right."

I hurried to the edge of the porch. "What's the matter?"

Blake walked up the steps, the puppy's tongue licking at his arm. "I think he's getting too attached to me. Every time I started to leave the pen, he would whine. So I thought I'd bring him with me for a few minutes. Maybe he'll settle down, and I'll take him back to the kennel."

I took him and sat back down in my chair, my arms cradling the dog against my body. "Come here, Astro. Do you miss Addie?"

The puppy's head rested on my arm, and his dark eyes stared up at me. I thought of what Ross said about Addie's hopes for the puppy. How could I fulfill Addie's dreams?

Perry stepped closer and held out the check again. "I have some carrier crates in the back of Celeste's car. George and I can take him and the others with us today."

I shook my head. "Addie wanted me to take care of them."

Perry slipped the check back in his pocket, repositioned the sunglasses on his face, and backed toward the steps. "You're taking on a big responsibility.

Think about it before you decide. I'll be out of town on business for the next few days, but Celeste will be home. Why don't you come over and look at our kennel? Maybe that will help you decide that we could better train the dogs than you."

Go over to Celeste's kennels? That would give me an opportunity to look around and see if there was anything to tie Celeste or Perry to Addie's death. "I'll do that. Tell Celeste I'll come tomorrow."

With a curt nod, Perry got in the Escalade, turned the ignition, and roared down the driveway. Flying pebbles from underneath his tires sprayed Blake's truck.

"Wow, he's in a hurry," Blake said. He stared at me for a minute and bit his bottom lip. "Well," he said, "I guess I'll get out of here and quit bothering you for today. See you in the morning."

As he started around the truck, I had the sinking feeling that he was walking out of my life. *Concentrate.* What could I do to make amends for changing the subject at breakfast? But on the other hand, I didn't want to appear like I was chasing him.

"Wait," I called just as he opened the door on the driver's side of his truck. I held the puppy close and flew down the steps and around the truck to where he stood. I stopped in front of him and gazed up. "You and Marcie have helped me so much since Addie's death. Why don't you pick her up and the two of you come back for supper tonight? I'll cook."

I couldn't believe those words were coming from my

mouth. I'd cook? My idea of fixing a meal was to defrost a frozen dinner in the microwave. I had no idea how to find my way around a kitchen except to scramble eggs or put bread in the toaster. That hardly qualified for a dinner meal.

Blake's eyes crinkled at the corner as a smile spread across his face. "I'd like that. Want us to bring anything?"

"No, I'll take care of everything."

"See you about six thirty?"

A sick feeling churned in my stomach. "Fine. See you then."

The truck drove away from the house. I looked at the puppy who still snuggled close to me. "Well, I've done it this time. I'll have to call and warn Marcie not to tell Blake how I've jumped into another situation without taking time to think. I haven't the foggiest notion of where to begin. Can you cook?"

The puppy licked my arm. "I didn't think so. I'll take you back to the kennel and then see what I can find in Addie's cookbooks. I wonder how long it takes to learn to cook."

At five thirty, I stood in the kitchen, hands on my hips, and tried not to feel too proud of my accomplishments. Addie always said pride was a dangerous enemy. It could knock you flat on your back when you were least expecting it.

But I had done it! I had fixed a meal that anybody could feel proud of, and I could hardly wait to see how impressed Blake and Marcie would be with my culinary skills.

I crossed my arms and smiled at the pot of bubbling spaghetti sauce and the water for the pasta that was just coming to a boil. Thank goodness for bottled sauce.

I reached for the package of spaghetti, unwrapped it, and dropped it in the boiling water. Would one be enough, or should I add another?

After dumping in a second container of pasta, I turned the stove down to simmer so the sauce and spaghetti would be ready by the time I completed my shower. A bagged salad which had been dumped in a large bowl sat in the fridge waiting to be served with the silver tongs I'd found in one of the drawers.

Frozen garlic bread lay on a cookie sheet ready to be shoved in the oven at the last minute, and a yummy cheesecake, fresh from Michaelson's Bakery, rounded out the meal. My willpower had kicked in as I removed the cake from the box, and I managed to keep from eating one of the strawberries that decorated the top of the cake.

Now all I had to do was grab a quick shower, get dressed, and greet my guests as the most gracious hostess they'd ever seen.

In the bathroom, I turned up my radio so I could hear the music over the running water. I sang at the top of my lungs right along with my favorite Christian rock group as I showered, dressed, and dried my hair.

When I slipped on my sandals, I caught sight of my bare feet.

"Oh dear, my toenails need to be painted."

Thirty minutes later, dressed, hair styled, and my toes with their new coat of nail polish peeking out of my sandals, I turned off the radio only to be greeted with the high-pitched blare of the downstairs fire alarm. I opened my bedroom door and was met with an overpowering smell of smoke.

With a scream, I bolted down the stairs.

In the kitchen, black smoke spiraled upward from the stove. A complete sense of helplessness started at my newly polished toenails and crawled upward, settling in my stomach, as I stared at the sight of the cooktop flames turned up high rather than on simmer.

Then my brain kicked into gear. I switched off the stove, grabbed an oven mitt, and set the pan with the sauce in the sink. I did the same with the spaghetti pot.

In disgust, I surveyed the crusted streaks of red and black which used to be sauce. The spaghetti lay charred in the bottom of the other pot. I turned on the faucet to fill the smoldering pans. "I wonder how long they'll have to soak before I can get that stuff out."

At that moment, the phone rang. I grabbed for it. "Hello."

"This is Security Central calling. Your fire alarm has gone off. We've dispatched emergency vehicles to your house."

"No," I screamed over the wail of the house alarm. "I burned something in the kitchen. Call them back. It's all right."

"Are you sure?"

"Yes, thank you."

I hung up and leaned against the kitchen cabinet, straining to hear sirens in the distance. But I heard nothing.

The main objective of the moment, however, was to get some fresh air into the house and get that alarm silenced. I ran to the back door and propped it open, then dashed through the house to the front door. I pushed it back and clapped my hand in horror over my mouth at how close I had come to smacking Blake in the face. All I could do was stand there, the smoke alarm still blaring, and stare at him and Marcie.

"What's the matter?" His nostrils flared as the burned smell poured from the house and engulfed the front porch.

Now how do I explain this?

"Would you give me a minute?" I said as I hurried back into the house. I reset the alarm and then returned to the porch. Blake looked as if he didn't have a clue what had happened, but I knew Marcie did.

She bit her lip and gave a little nod—the signal she'd always used to let me know she understood my feelings. Her support bolstered my courage.

There was no escaping it. I had to tell Blake my secret. I took a deep breath and straightened my shoulders. "Well, Blake," I said, "I guess you've just discovered what Marcie's always known. I'm ADD."

Blake frowned. "You have Attention Deficit Disorder?"

"Yeah, but mine's worse. I'm also an Automatic Disaster Detonator. Everywhere I go, trouble follows me. Even in the kitchen."

The shocked look that had been on Blake's face when I opened the door dissolved as he burst into laughter. "Oh, Leigh, you crack me up. Tell us what happened."

There was no turning back. I had to tell him the secret that only Marcie knew. "The thing is, I can't concentrate on anything for more than a minute at a time. I knew I couldn't cook, but I just opened my mouth and out came the invitation. I do things like that all the time."

He smiled. "And?"

"And I meant to turn the stove down, but I turned it up, and then I went to take a shower, and then—"

"Listen to me," he interrupted. "I don't care about dinner. I don't care if you get distracted or not. The thing is, you make me laugh and bring me more happiness than I've had in a long time."

"Really?" I couldn't believe my ears.

"Yeah, I knew you were special the day you sang that solo with the choir at church. I felt so sorry for you when you choked. You tried so hard to keep singing between those hacking coughs."

Now I really felt like a fraud. "You're going to think I'm a terrible person."

"Why?"

A hiccup shook my body. "I wasn't choking. I forgot the words, and I covered it up by pretending to cough."

It only took a second for his reaction. His laughter rang out across the porch. "What a smart thing to do. I would never have thought of that. I would have stood there looking like an idiot. You had everybody in the church feeling sorry for you."

"But I'm just a big fake."

"No, you're not," Marcie interrupted. "Blake's telling you exactly what I've been saying for years. Maybe you'll believe me now."

Marcie had been so quiet I'd almost forgotten she was there. I smiled at her. "Thanks, Marcie. I don't know what I would have done without you."

She glanced back into the house. "Well, the smoke seems to have cleared out. Let's get your kitchen cleaned up."

"Oh, there's no need for that," I protested. "I'll take care of it."

Blake shook his head. "No, we'll all do it. Then we can go over to the Dairy Bar and get some burgers and shakes." I smiled. "That sounds good. I really don't like to clean, so I'd appreciate the help."

He burst out laughing and regarded me with a hint of skepticism. "Oh no. A woman with ADD that can't cook and hates to clean. Do you have any more secrets?"

"Not that I know of."

"Good. Now let's get that kitchen cleaned."

I led the way inside but stopped in horror at the kitchen door. The water ran full force from the faucet, just as it had when I turned it on. The pots which were blocking the drain had filled, and now the water cascaded over the side of the sink to the floor. A small river flowed across the linoleum.

I let out a yelp and ran for the sink. My foot slipped in the water, and I skidded into the cabinet but managed to grab the faucet handle and turn off the water.

I leaned against the sink, the water wetting the front of my shirt. "What else is going to happen?"

Blake stared at the puddle then smiled. "Looks like we have a bigger mess than I thought. I'll run down to your workshop and get the shop vac from there. We'll have this water cleared in no time."

"Thanks," I said as he went out the back door. A warning bell chimed in my mind, and I sank down in a chair at the table.

Marcie sloshed over and sat across from me. "That Blake sure is a nice guy, isn't he?"

"Yeah," I whispered. The bell in my head clanged louder bringing a thought I'd rather not acknowledge.

How did Blake know I kept the shop vac in my workshop? Maybe he saw it when he was getting my mortise chisel.

9

My eyes blinked open the next morning at the bright rays of sunlight pouring through the windows of my bedroom. My body stretched in an effort to chase the remnants of sleep. The muscles in my back and arms ached at the sudden movement, a reminder of my unfamiliar experience of scrubbing the kitchen the night before.

My laced fingers slipped through my hair and propped my head on the pillow. The changing patterns of light danced above me on the ceiling, bringing a smile to my lips. My heartbeat increased with the memory of the night before. True to his word, Blake worked right alongside Marcie and me as we tried to restore the kitchen to its original state.

Splotches of spaghetti sauce had decorated the wall and floor surrounding the stove, and I even discovered some on the refrigerator door on the other side of the room.

"That pan of sauce must have bubbled like Old Faithful," I said as I swung my legs over the side of the bed and started to get up.

I glanced at the floor and frowned. The bedroom slippers that should have been on the floor beside my bed were nowhere in sight. A quick search revealed one next to the chair by the window and the other by the dresser across the room. How they got there I had no idea.

I sighed and stared at my reflection in the dresser mirror. "Just another normal day in the life of Leigh Dennison, armchair detective. I don't think Lt. Green would be too impressed with my detective skills."

My list of suspects seemed to grow each day, but so far I'd found out nothing helpful. Preacher Cochran had a violent past and had been seen holding the murder weapon, Ross James argued with Addie and disappeared with money he said Addie gave him, Celeste and Perry Witherington wanted the dogs, and Blake. . . What about him? He needed money for his father's medical bills, he'd been alone on the porch, and he knew where the shop vac was kept. I had nothing in the way of substantial evidence on anyone.

Doubts flooded into my mind. What made me think I could solve this murder? I couldn't even manage to cook dinner. I felt so alone and helpless. I'd experienced that feeling many times in my life, and I knew where to turn. I dropped to my knees.

"Thank you, God, for letting me know and love Addie, and I pray You'll make me more like her. Be with me as I try to find who took her life. I give You the praise for what You're going to do in my life. Thank You for caring for me even when I'm not worthy. Amen."

A new resolve to face whatever challenges might come my way flowed through me as I arose. What I needed was a cup of coffee.

Ten minutes later, I poured myself the first cup of the day and prepared to settle down in the den to watch *The Today Show*. As the opening music announced the show, howls rose from the direction of the kennel. Those dogs were at it again. A glance at the clock told me it would be another half hour before Blake would arrive. If anyone was going to answer the call of the wild, it would be me.

I slammed out the back door and stomped across the yard that led to the kennel area, the thought of my untouched coffee uppermost in my mind. I could hardly believe what I saw. Preacher Cochran squatted outside the fence to the exercise area of the kennel. Beau and Belle stood on the other side, their noses pressed to the fence and their tails wagging.

"What are you doing?"

Preacher jumped to his feet and whirled to face me. "I ain't doin' nothing but talkin' to my little buddies."

"You scared me. I thought something was wrong with the dogs." I clutched my robe around me and directed what I hoped was a menacing look his way.

He shook his head. "I know you ain't never liked me. 'Course I can't figure out what I ever done to you. You sure ain't as nice as Miss Addie was."

His words hit me almost like a slap in the face. My hand on my robe tightened, and I stood there speechless. I had just prayed that God would make me more like Addie. Now a homeless man was telling me I didn't treat people the way Addie did.

His shoulders sagged a little, and he glanced back down at the dogs. "It ain't far through the field over to my bridge. I can hear them howlin', and it worries me. I just can't figure out why they're cryin' like that. They never done that before."

I had to admit that Beau and Belle hadn't been half as playful since Addie's death.

"They've been upset ever since Addie died. I think they miss her a lot." Another thought flashed through my mind. "Have you been coming to see them when I wasn't here?"

He shifted his weight from one foot to another. "Yeah, but don't worry. I ain't been back in your workshop. I just wanted to visit with my little buddies. I been worried about them."

I gazed at the dogs inside the pen. They stood together on the other side of the fence, but the animation I had seen on their faces in the past was no longer there. I walked inside the exercise yard, picked up the puppy, and held him close. Beau and Belle, who used to be in almost perpetual motion, turned away and lay down next to the fence on the other side of the yard.

Preacher pointed to the parents. "See, they ain't acting right."

"I know, but I can't figure it out."

"Maybe you need to ask somebody that raises Norwich terriers. Miss Addie loved her dogs, and I can't stand to hear them cry like they been doin'."

With a sigh I put the puppy down and joined Preacher outside the gate. "Addie wanted me to take care of the dogs, but I don't know how. Celeste and Perry Witherington want to buy them. Maybe it would be best for me to sell."

Preacher's eyes grew wide. "To *that* woman? She don't know nothin' about dogs like Miss Addie did. You can't sell 'em to her."

"But I can't run this place alone." I turned back to Preacher. "Now if you'll excuse me I've got work to do this morning."

Preacher drew himself up to his full height. "You don't have to worry about me no more. I 'spect it's about time for me to move on. I'll be headin' out of here in a few days."

He turned and holding his head erect walked across the field on the way back to his bridge. His words left me shaken. He couldn't leave until I knew whether or not he'd killed Addie. And surely the police wouldn't let him go—that is, if they knew what he was planning. Maybe I needed to tell them.

A familiar bark sounded at the side of the house. Blake with Red at his side walked toward me. When Red caught sight of me, he bounded across the yard and stopped in front of me, his tail swishing back and forth across his back and his deep-set eyes staring up at me.

I dropped to my knees and wrapped my arms around his neck. His tongue licked at my face. "Good morning, Red," I said with a laugh, "it's good to see you."

Blake stopped in front of me. "Are you glad to see me, too?"

I stood up and placed my hands on my hips. "I don't know. He seems happier to see me than you do."

Blake laughed. "Don't let my shy nature deceive

you. I'm a tiger at heart."

"Well, tiger," I said, "I've got a busy day. I'm going over to Celeste Witherington's."

"What for?"

"Just to see how she runs her kennel." I didn't want him to know that it was really a sleuthing trip.

"I wish I could go with you, but I promised the principal I would come to the school this morning. I help out in the summer when he's doing the fall schedules. It'll probably take most of the day."

"Well, I'll see you later. Want me to fix you some breakfast while you're feeding the dogs?"

A loud laugh burst from his mouth. "You've got to be kidding. After last night? Coffee will be fine."

I swatted his arm, laughed, and headed to the house. The more I saw of Blake, the deeper my feelings for him grew. But until that one doubt was erased, I knew there was no future for us.

Several hours later, I stopped in Celeste Witherington's driveway behind a car with a Tennessee license plate on the back. My eyes widened in amazement at the steep pitched roof and dormers of the rambling house before me. The French-style chateau with its half-timbered and stone walls reminded me of a scaled imitation of the mansion on the Biltmore Estate at Asheville. French Normandy architecture seemed to fit right in with Celeste's personality.

"You need any help?" The voice drifted from the plants next to the house.

The leaves on the tall boxwoods stirred as George Daniels walked from behind them and stopped at the edge of the driveway. Pruning shears dangled from his right hand, and a handkerchief in his left hand mopped the perspiration standing on his forehead. The evidence of long hours in the sun could be seen in his tanned skin.

"Good morning, Mr. Daniels. I'm Leigh Dennison. I met you the other day at my home."

"Good to see you again, Miss Dennison. You caught me in the middle of some gardening."

"Are you the gardener? I thought you helped with the dogs."

He wiped his forehead again. "I guess you could say I'm just a jack-of-all-trades around here."

My gaze traveled over the well-kept yard with its shrubs and flowering plants displayed in artistically designed beds. "You've done an amazing job. I've never seen such gorgeous flowers."

George's chest seemed to puff out. "Thanks. I love plants. Can't stand to be inside. When the weather's good and the dogs are taken care of, I want to be out and diggin' in the dirt."

"I'm sure Celeste is very proud of what you've created here."

George gave a little grunt. "Don't know about that. At least Mr. Perry is."

"Perry said you've worked for his family for years."

"I worked for his daddy, Mr. Paul, when Mr. Perry was just a baby. Been with 'em ever since. His daddy was a fine man."

I smiled at him. "I'm sure Celeste was glad to have your experience after her husband died."

The man's forehead crinkled in a frown. "I stayed for Mr. Perry. He couldn't come back home then because of his job. Mr. Perry's never been close to Celeste, and he asked me to stay on until he could get some business deals closed. I did it for him."

"Your loyalty to the family is admirable—helping with the kennel, taking care of the grounds. I'm sure they couldn't do without you."

He smiled and tucked his handkerchief in his pocket. "Well, I do whatever I can to help out."

I frowned and moved a little closer to George. "Tell me, was Perry's father traveling in France when he met Celeste?"

George's eyes widened. "France? She's not from France. She grew up in a little coal mining town in Kentucky. Mr. Paul met her in Nashville where she was working at the time."

Now that was a surprise. Celeste was about as continental as French toast.

"I'm sure you know that I'm the new owner of Jordan's Kennels. I thought I'd come over and get some advice from Celeste on how to run a kennel."

George laid the shears he was still holding on the ground. "Then you really ought to talk to Mr. Perry, but he's not here today. Had to go to Asheville. He's in charge now that he's back in town."

This was getting more interesting by the moment. "Really?" George was just a wealth of information. Maybe he would keep talking and tell me more.

"Yeah. 'Course Mr. Perry don't know too much about dogs—nothing like his daddy did. But Mr. Perry's a businessman. He's ready for this kennel to produce some winners in the ring."

"I see."

George smiled and leaned closer to me. "That's why Mr. Perry wants some new breeding stock, and he's willing to pay top dollar."

"He sure seems to want Addie's puppy."

"Yeah, but only if you want to sell. Don't be put off by his insistence. That's just the businessman in him coming out."

"I'll remember that, George." A thought flashed in my mind. "Did Addie know Perry?"

George wrinkled his brow and thought for a moment. "I don't think so. But she sure would have liked him if she'd ever met him."

I remembered Perry's piercing gaze and the smile that seemed to be directed only to me. "I'm sure she would have."

George stared into space for a moment. "Yeah, Miss Addie would like the changes Perry is making around here." He chuckled. "He's sure put a halt to some of Celeste's spending sprees."

I looked around. "Where is Celeste now?"

George motioned to a flagstone pathway that lay

next to the house. "Follow that, and you'll come to the kennels. There's a couple from Tennessee down there with her now."

I thanked him and headed around the side of the house. The first glimpse of Celeste's kennels brought me to a full stop. The pens stretched along the length of a gravel drive that seemed to originate at a dilapidated barn about five hundred yards in back of the kennel area. A four-wheeler stood in front of the pens, a bag of dog food perched behind the driver's seat.

Dogs lay sprawled in the small exercise area of each of the pens. One quick glance told me the quarters weren't as neat as Addie's. Perhaps it was cleaner when Perry Witherington was present. The absence of barking concerned me, for I had listened to Addie's dogs for days and wondered why these seemed so quiet.

Celeste appeared deep in conversation with a young man and woman as I approached. The young woman held a puppy in her arms, and the man's attention centered on Celeste. I stopped several yards behind Celeste, the couple facing me. They glanced at me as I came to a stop several feet behind Celeste, and she turned. Her eyes lit up when she saw me.

"Oh, chérie, I'll be with you in a few minutes."

Celeste turned back to the couple and shook her head at the young man. "No, I never give out my customers' names. I couldn't release that confidential information without their authorization."

Strange words to be coming from a reputable breeder. Addie always told me a good breeder's business was built on the satisfaction of former clients, and she kept a list of names and phone numbers of everyone who had ever bought from her. In fact she encouraged interested buyers to check her out with past customers.

The young man frowned. "What kind of guarantee do you offer on your puppies?"

Celeste's hand touched the bun on the back of her head, and she smoothed her blond hair into place. "My guarantee covers the first visit to the vet."

A warning flashed through my mind. I had seen Addie's written guarantees many times. She advised prospective buyers about any hereditary problems that might arise with the dog and offered a full refund if that occurred. She always discussed at length the general health problems of Norwich terriers before a puppy left her kennel, but I wasn't hearing the same thing from Celeste.

The young man glanced at the woman by his side. "Well, may we see the puppy's mother?"

"I'm afraid that's impossible. She's at the vet's office today having a check-up. But I can e-mail you a picture of her if you like." Celeste's voice dripped with honey.

Another warning sign. Addie always showed buyers the parents of a puppy. I had often heard her on the phone, advising people interested in purchasing a dog about the importance of seeing the mother and father.

The man reached over, took the puppy from the woman's arms, and handed it to Celeste. "Thank you for your time, Mrs. Witherington. I think we've seen enough to know we're not interested in purchasing one of your animals. Good day."

With that they brushed past me and walked in the direction of their car. Celeste stood still for a moment before she slowly turned. She glanced in the direction of the departing customers, took a deep breath, and smiled at me.

"Chérie, I'm so glad you came today."

I stepped forward and patted the puppy she held. "What a cute little fellow."

Celeste glanced down at the puppy, turned, and opened the pen behind her. The puppy tumbled from her arms and hit the ground with a thud. Without a backward glance she locked the gate and faced me. "Have you decided to sell, Leigh?"

My gaze followed the puppy's progress as he hobbled across the pen, his short legs trembling. I gave my head a little shake, blinked before turning to Celeste, and forced a big smile.

"No, I'm keeping the dogs. I just came over today to get a look at your kennel. You know, as one breeder to another."

Celeste's face turned crimson. "But, Leigh, you know nothing about taking care of dogs. They would be much better off here with us than with you."

"I don't know about that, Celeste. I've become quite attached to the dogs. I may hire me a trainer to continue with Labelle. In fact, I'm looking forward to hitting the dog show circuit."

The sun beat down on my head, and I wondered if I was running a fever. There were only two possibilities that could cause me to make such rash statements—I was either suffering from heat stroke or the ADD had finally destroyed my brain.

Celeste's lips tightened across her teeth. "You're making a big mistake, Leigh."

"Maybe so, but it's my decision. Thanks for the offer, but no thanks, Celeste. I'll see you in the show ring."

Still in shock over my sudden decision, I wobbled back up the flagstone walkway. I relaxed with relief to be away from the kennel so unlike Addie's. And then it dawned on me. It wasn't Addie's kennel anymore. It was mine. And I had one big problem.

Where was I going to find a trainer to get Astro ready for the show ring?

10

During the hour drive back from Macon Falls, I thought about my spur-of-the-minute decision. How typical of me to jump into something without really thinking about what I would do. Blake would be returning to school in a few weeks, and Marcie couldn't run my shop forever. Before I found a trainer, I had to come up with someone to help me care for the dogs.

Why not Preacher Cochran? I could ask him to come help me at the kennels. He'd helped Addie enough, and he knew what to do. I could tell him I needed someone to watch after Addie's dogs for me, and maybe that would keep him from leaving until I could find out whether or not he was the murderer.

There was just one problem. I'd promised Blake I wouldn't go back to see Preacher alone. If Blake was finished with the schedules, he could go with me. I drove past the bridge where Preacher lived but didn't stop.

Just before I reached the drive leading to my house, the truck jerked, and a backfire shattered the air. Almost as if I willed the truck up the winding entrance to the farm, it inched along, sputtering as it went, and finally stopped at the front door of the house. I sat there, my hands grasping the steering wheel. At least I'd made it home.

The dogs in the kennel picked that time to begin

their barking, and their howls rang out across the still afternoon. The sound served as a reminder of what I'd said to Celeste earlier. Hit the dog show circuit? Me? It was laughable.

I entered the house and rushed to the study to look up the name of the mechanic Addie used. The beep of the answering machine signaled that I had a message.

A quick check of the instrument brought a smile to my lips at the drawl of Blake's voice on the recording. "Leigh, wanted to let you know we need dog food. I'm still working in the principal's office on the fall schedules, and I'm gonna be tied up for a while. If you can, run into town and pick up a couple of bags at the vet's office. Oh, and by the way, I'd like to take you to dinner tonight. How about trying that new restaurant on the river just outside of town? See ya later."

I reached for the receiver to call him back, but the phone rang. The caller ID flashed a number outside our area code. "Hello."

"Hello." The voice was unfamiliar. "This is Marcus Turnbow. I'm calling in regard to Mrs. Jordan."

A smile pulled at my lips. "Mr. Turnbow, this is Leigh Dennison. I've never met you, but I've heard Addie mention you many times."

There was a pause on the other end of the line. "I'm a breeder from the Atlanta area and a good friend of Addie's. I've just returned from a trip to Europe, and I heard about her death. I can't believe that she was murdered. I wanted to call and express my sympathy and see if there's anything I can do to help."

"Thank you. I'm living in Addie's house now and trying to see that her dogs are taken care of."

"She'd certainly want you to do that. She loved her dogs."

"She told me many times how you two were competitors in the show ring."

He laughed. "Yes, but only in group. I breed and train Norfolk terriers, a little different from the Norwich. We often met in the group competition at shows after our dogs had each won their best of breed class. I respected her greatly as a breeder, as a trainer, but most of all as one of the best people I've ever had the privilege to know."

"Thank you, Mr. Turnbow, I appreciate that more than you'll ever know."

There was silence for a moment, and then he cleared his throat. "What about her dogs? Is the puppy okay? I know Addie had great hopes for him."

"They're fine, just having some trouble adjusting to life without Addie, but so am I. She left her estate to me, including the dogs. I don't know what I'm going to do about them."

"Well, I hope you'll do what Addie wanted, continue to train and show them."

"Show them?" I felt my eyes grow wide. "I don't know the first thing about training a dog. I could never show them. Celeste Witherington has been after me to sell them to her, but I can't bring myself to do it."

"I should hope not," he muttered. "That woman doesn't run a kennel. She has a puppy mill. Addie would never want Celeste to have any of her dogs."

"But I thought she was successful in the show ring. She's had some dogs become champions."

Marcus gave a little laugh. "She sure has, but they've never been dogs she's bred. She'll buy a dog from a breeder, maybe in Europe, farm him out to a good trainer, and then show up at the competitions to take the praise if he wins. She doesn't know the first thing about training dogs."

I sighed. "Well, I don't either. I could never get Addie's dogs ready for the show ring."

"Oh yes, you could," he said. "In fact, you've got the perfect person to help you. Addie trained her helper Ross. He knows what to do."

"Well," I faltered, "Ross is busy taking care of his ill mother right now."

"That's too bad, Miss Dennison. He's a natural. I've watched him with Addie's dogs at shows. He's still got a lot to learn, but maybe the two of you could do that together."

"I don't know. I'd have to think about that."

"I'd be glad to help any way I can for Addie's sake. If you want me to help you find a good trainer, let me know. The new season will be starting soon, and the puppy needs to be entered in his eligible classes for experience. I'd sure hate to see him not get his chance."

"We'll see. But I do appreciate your call, Mr. Turnbow."

"Good to talk to you, and please call me if you

need me. I'm sure Addie has my number in her business files."

"Good-bye, and thanks for calling."

I cradled the phone as the line disconnected. Our conversation replayed in my mind. It seemed I was in the minority. Everybody—Blake, Mr. Turnbow, and even Addie—thought Ross showed a lot of promise. Maybe I should give some thought to letting him come back to work.

I replaced the phone and remembered Blake's message, the most important one to my way of thinking.

Dog food and a mechanic were the priorities now. My truck probably wouldn't make the trip into town. In fact, it needed to be towed to the garage. A quick check in Addie's address book gave me the name of the garage I needed to call. *But it could be hours before they can come get my truck.*

A thought struck me. Addie's truck. It had been parked in the kennel garage ever since the police returned it after looking it over. If I drove it into town, I could stop at the garage and ask them to pick up my truck. "But what did the police do with the key?"

I ran from the house and toward the garage. When I climbed in the truck, the keys still hung in the ignition. The engine cranked right away, and I drove toward town. My eyes scanned the bridge area on my way by, but Preacher was still nowhere to be seen.

An hour later, with the dog food in the back of the truck and the mechanic's assurance that he would tow my pickup, I drove to the high school. Blake's truck sat in the faculty parking area. On impulse, I decided to stop and find out what time we'd be going to dinner. Another vehicle sat beside Blake's, the same truck that was in the driveway when we visited Ross.

The deserted halls of the school looked the same as they did ten years before when Marcie and I were seniors. Custodial supplies lined the halls, an indication of the summer clean-up, but I didn't see anyone working. The click of my heels echoed through the empty building as I walked into the reception area of the principal's office. Not even the secretary was present today, but I could hear Blake's voice drifting through the open door of her office.

"I don't know if Leigh will agree to that, Ross," I heard Blake say.

"Please talk to her, Mr. Cameron. She'll listen to you." Ross's voice held a pleading tone.

"Agree to what?" I asked as I stepped into the room.

Blake and Ross turned in surprise, and Blake's mouth curved into a smile. The brows above Ross's eyes pulled down in a frown. "Leigh." Blake stood up from his perch on the office desk. "I didn't expect you to come by here."

I walked over to where the two of them stood. "I came into town to get the dog food and thought I'd stop by. What are you two talking about?"

Blake glanced at Ross and cleared his throat. "Ross needs a job, Leigh, and nobody in town is willing to give him a chance until Addie's murder is solved. He's really good with the dogs, and you need somebody to help you when I go back to school. We were wondering if you'd give him a chance to come back to work at the kennel."

Thoughts rushed through my mind. Marcus Turnbow had suggested the perfect reason for Ross to come back to the kennels. If Ross thought he was needed to help me with the puppy, one of my chief suspects would be under surveillance at all times. Maybe he would slip up and reveal something undiscovered as of yet. On the other hand, if he was a murderer, I might be placing myself in danger.

But I had to find out who killed Addie. Maybe having Ross close by wasn't a bad idea.

"All right, Ross. I'll give you another chance. In fact, I had a call from Marcus Turnbow today. He told me with the new season coming up, you're the perfect one to train the puppy for competition. Why don't you start in the morning? You can begin by working your regular hours with the same pay if that's agreeable." I could hardly believe what I'd just said.

His eyes grew wide, and a huge smile covered his face. "Oh, thank you, Miss Dennison. You won't be sorry. I'll take care of those dogs just like Miss Addie taught me, and I'll do everything I can to get Astro ready for the show ring. You can depend on that."

He started for the door but stopped and looked at Blake. "Thank you, Mr. Cameron. You're the best."

Blake waved his hand in dismissal, and the boy disappeared out the door. Blake looked at me, a smile on his lips. "Thanks for helping him, Leigh."

"We'll see how things work out, but I want you to know I still have my doubts about him."

Blake smiled. "But at least you're willing to give him a chance."

My reason for wanting to talk to Blake popped into my mind. "When will you be finished here?"

"The principal had to run an errand, and I was just finishing up when Ross walked in. Why?"

"I wanted to go back out to talk to Preacher, and I wondered if you'd go along."

"Sure." He picked up a stack of papers. "Let me run these down to the guidance counselor's office, and I'll be ready to go."

"I'll meet you outside." I started toward the door but glanced over my shoulder. "By the way, I'm using Addie's truck. I'm having trouble with mine."

"I'll follow you out to the bridge. Then I'll be by later to take you to dinner."

As I walked from the school, I tried to remember if I turned the washer on before leaving home this morning. I glanced at my watch. If I didn't, there should be enough time once I got home to do that load of laundry before Blake arrived.

So engrossed was I in what I was thinking that my mind wasn't concentrating on the task at present. Just as I opened the door to the truck and started to get in, the keys slipped from my fingers, hit the floor, and bounced back under the driver's seat.

"Oh, good grief." I bent over and stuck my hand

up under the seat, my fingers groping across the area for my keys. My hand made contact with the metal and pulled them forward. I raked the keys from underneath, and a wadded up piece of paper rolled out with them.

"What could this be?" I grasped the paper in both hands and smoothed the crumpled form. My breath caught in my throat.

This was no ordinary piece of paper. The check bore the logo of the St. Claire First Community Bank, and was made out to Jordan's Kennels, signed by the woman who had bought Bud and Teenie's last puppy.

The check was in the deposit I helped Addie with. I had endorsed and added it to the total. How did it get here?

How could the police have overlooked something like this? Had it been there when they examined the truck, or was it placed there later?

I tried to remember who had driven the truck before the police took it for examination. Ross had gone to Cherokee, and the police had driven it to the garage when they brought it home.

Solving the mystery of Addie's death was not getting any easier. If anything, each day brought something new to confuse me.

———

Blake followed me all the way to the bridge. Each time I glanced in the rearview mirror my heart ached at the thought that I had such doubts about him.

When we pulled up next to Preacher's campsite, we both got out. I shaded my eyes and peered around for the Vietnam vet, but I didn't see him anywhere.

"Preacher!" Blake called out.

No answer. There was no sign of life anywhere up and down the riverbank.

"Preacher!"

Still no answer.

The items underneath the bridge caught my attention. Curiosity overcame me. Maybe I could find something there that would link Preacher to Addie's death. I walked to the bridge support and stared inside at Preacher's earthly goods.

Blake walked up beside me. "What are you doing?"

My hand reached out toward the first stack against the supports, but I drew back. These items belonged to someone else. "I'd like to search Preacher's belongings, but I can't bring myself to do it."

In the dim light under the bridge, I could see an open suitcase. It appeared to contain clothing.

Preacher's fishing rod and equipment lay next to some pots and pans. An overturned sack spilled canned meats and vegetables across the ground. Some empty cans lay scattered about, but there appeared to be no burned area where Preacher cooked his meals. Apparently, he ate his meals cold.

For the first time my heart realized what Addie must have seen when she came to the bridge—a man without a home, family, or even the small comforts of life. How that must have touched her.

Blake tapped my arm. "Let's go, Leigh. We'll come back when he's here."

I turned to leave, but my eye caught sight of a stack of books lying just underneath the bridge. "I wonder what kind of books he reads."

I leaned over to get a better view and clamped my hand over my mouth to keep from crying out. Was I really seeing what lay before me, or was it a duplicate of something I knew so well?

The word *Mother* was inscribed on the front of a leather-bound volume with the words Holy Bible just above. How many times had I seen that book? I could quote the words written inside without looking. *To Mom. Until we meet again. Your loving son, Charles.*

I clamped my hand over my mouth to keep from crying out. No one, not even me, realized Addie's Bible, her greatest treasure, was missing. Preacher must have taken it when he killed her for she would never have parted with the last gift her son gave her before leaving for Vietnam.

"Leigh?" Blake said. "What's wrong?"

I took a deep breath and pointed to the Bible. "That's Addie's Bible."

He stared down at it. "Why would Preacher have it?"

"I don't know."

"What 'cha want now?" a voice behind us growled.

We turned to see Preacher glaring at us. I grabbed Blake's arm. "We just came by to see if you'd left yet."

He shook his head. "Don't guess I'll be doin' that for a while. The police told me not to."

I pulled Blake toward the trucks. "Well, we'll check on you again. Bye."

"Come anytime," Preacher said as we left.

When we got back to the truck, Blake opened the door for me. "Leigh, we've got to go to the police with this."

"Can we talk about this at dinner?"

"Okay, but we've got to take this to Detective Sawyer."

I knew Blake was right. There was a lot I needed to tell Detective Sawyer—the whereabouts of Addie's Bible, the check underneath the seat, Celeste's interest in the dogs, and my suspicions about Blake. I couldn't keep my discoveries to myself any longer. It was time to come clean with the police.

11

I waited for Blake to pull out from Preacher's campsite and disappear down the road before I turned toward town. Whenever I had a problem, Marcie always came to mind. She had a gift for sifting through conflicting information and coming up with the right answer. At that moment, I wanted to talk to my friend more than anything in the world. I glanced at my watch. The shop would be open for another hour. I headed toward Dennison's Treasure Chest.

The familiar Escalade sat in the parking lot of the shop. A groan escaped my lips. Although Celeste mentioned she wanted to come to my little shop, as she called it, her presence surprised me.

"Oh, great. The ending to a perfect day. All I need is for her to start asking to buy the dogs again."

Inside the shop, Celeste struggled to get a large oil painting out the front door. Her eyes widened when she saw me, and then her lips curled in a smile.

"Chérie." She repositioned the painting to get a better hold. "I finally made it to your little shop, and I must say I'm pleased with your inventory. I would have come sooner if I had known what quality antiques you have."

My eyes took in the back of the canvas she held. "Did you find something you liked?"

She turned the painting so I could see it. "Oui, I've

purchased this beautiful oil painting of these Yorkshire terriers. It's the most gorgeous work I've seen in a long time."

I sucked in my breath at the painting she held. "Well, thank you for your business, Celeste. That's a very expensive piece. I hope you enjoy it."

"Oh, I will, chérie. I have the perfect place to hang it. And if you change your mind about selling me the dogs, let me know." She glanced around the shop. "I don't know how you have time to take care of them with having to work in your shop."

"Marcie helps me out a lot. In fact she's about running the place until I find out who killed Addie."

Concern flashed in her eyes. "Be careful. You need to let the police find out who murdered my sweet friend. Don't do anything to put yourself in danger."

I smiled at her. "Don't worry. I've uncovered some things that may help me put an end to this before long."

"Well, think about my offer for the dogs." She juggled the painting in an effort to open the door, but I reached out and held it open for her to exit. She glanced over her shoulder as she stepped outside and smiled. "*Au revoir* for now."

I watched until she had stowed the painting in the back of her SUV and then walked toward Marcie who stood next to the cash register. "I can't believe she bought that painting. What was the price on it? Fifteen hundred dollars?"

Marcie laughed. "Yes. I've heard you talk about

her, but I'd never met her. She came in, looked around for a little while, and then decided on that piece. She pulled out a wad of bills and paid cash for it."

I rubbed my hands together. "Well, Marcie, we don't have to worry about paying the electric bill this month."

We both laughed and grabbed each other in a big hug. Marcie held me at arms' length. "Now tell me what brings you here this late in the day."

For the next few minutes, I told her about my day and what I'd learned. When I finished, she regarded me with serious eyes. "Blake's right. You've got to tell John about this right away."

"John?" I asked in surprise.

Her cheeks turned crimson. "Well, he's been in here several times lately. He seems like a really nice guy. And he's working hard to find Addie's killer."

"Nice, huh?"

Marcie smiled. "He really is. Why don't you talk to him? You'll see."

"Maybe I will."

—

By the time I arrived home and pulled up in front of the house, it was six o'clock. Loud barking rang out from the direction of the kennel. With a sigh I released the brake and guided the truck around the drive to the back of the house and stopped at the kennels.

Beau, Belle, and Astro stood at the fence of the

exercise area, their heads back, and their voices raised. Bud and Teenie in the pen next to them joined in the chorus.

I got out of the truck and dropped to my knees outside the fence. Their full food bowls made me wonder if they'd eaten anything all day.

"What's the matter, guys?"

Beau and Belle whined and huddled closer together, and Astro tried to stick his nose through the fence toward me. The emptiness they surely were experiencing over Addie's death left me feeling just as lost as they looked.

I wiggled my fingers through the fence at them. "I guess you and I share something, little fellas."

The three licked at my fingers. I stood up, unlocked the gate, and stepped inside the kennel yard. As I squatted down, they jumped on my leg and licked at my hands. I picked up Beau, held him close to my body, and stroked his head.

Belle barked as if requesting her turn. She reacted the same way as he did, and a glimmer of love for these little creatures stirred in my soul.

Astro whined as if requesting his turn, and I set down Belle and picked him up. I could feel the beat of his heart against my arm, and I suddenly realized these little animals that relied on others for their care could be a great source of love to those who would open their hearts.

A whimper caught my attention, and I glanced down at the dark eyes that gazed up at me. Astro burrowed his nose into the crook of my arm. "Don't worry, little fellow. I'll take care of you."

With Astro in my arms, I walked from the kennel, pulled the truck in the garage, and left Astro inside the vehicle while I unloaded the bags bought at the vet's office. A search of a storage cabinet nearby yielded a small plastic container which I filled with enough dog food to get the puppy through the night. The puppy, his front feet propped on the inside of the truck's door, peered at me through the open window.

I reached through and picked him up. "Come on, Astro, you're going to spend the night with me."

The puppy relaxed in my arms and didn't move a muscle on the walk to the house and into the kitchen. Once inside I set him on the floor while I poured the food in one bowl and water in another. When I placed them in front of him, he inched toward the containers and sniffed at the contents.

"Go on, boy."

He looked up at me, back at the bowls, and then attacked them with a vengeance. He gobbled the food and lapped the water as if he hadn't eaten in days. Perhaps he was starving.

The ringing of my cell phone interrupted my thoughts, and I pulled it from my pocket. "Hello."

"Leigh," Blake's voice came over the line. "I'm afraid I'm going to have to take a rain check on dinner tonight."

"Why?"

"I'm sorry. We're not through with these schedules

yet. We think if we can work about three more hours we can get it done. We'll just grab some burgers at the Dairy Bar and keep working till we're finished."

The puppy's soft body rubbed against my leg. "That's okay. I have another male to keep me company tonight."

"What did you say?"

The surprise in Blake's voice made me giggle. "Yeah, I guess I'll just curl up on my couch and wrap my arms around this cute fellow. In fact as soon as he's house-trained I may even let him move in with me."

A laugh sounded on the other end of the line. "I'm beginning to think the female is the fickle one. First it's Red, now it's someone else."

"Oh, Blake, he's the sweetest little thing." The puppy lay snuggled next to my feet. I squatted down and caressed his back. "The dogs were barking again when I got home. I've brought Astro inside, and I'll probably keep him here until I can figure out what's wrong with them."

"Where's he gonna sleep?"

"There's a pet crate on the back porch. Addie used it for transporting the dogs to shows. I'll let him sleep in there until he's housebroken."

"That's good. I wish I could be with you tonight."

A hint of worry in his voice caused me to sit up straight. "Blake, is something wrong?"

"I hope not."

"What is it?"

"My mother called today. My dad isn't doing too

well. The doctor ran some more tests."

I rubbed my arm at the sudden chill his words produced. "Will this cause them more financial worries?"

"I don't think so. They found the money to pay all their bills, so they should be all right."

My heart felt as if it plummeted to the bottom of my stomach. Could Addie's money have paid off those bills? I struggled to speak. "Wh–what do they think it is?"

"They suspect a few things, but no definite diagnosis yet. I may have to go home for a few days."

"Yes, of course. But I'm sure it's nothing serious."

"I hope not." Blake sighed. "Anyway, you have a good night. I'll be by first thing in the morning."

"Thanks, and don't work too hard."

I set down the phone, my mind racing. Maybe Blake had used the money from the deposit to pay his father's medical bills and was looking for an excuse now to get out of town.

I thought of my parents and remembered how devastated I'd been when they died. The puppy rubbed against my leg, and I looked down at him. "It's just you and me, kid. Let me see what I can rustle up for my dinner."

Several hours later I sat curled up on the den sofa, eating my dinner—a bowl of cereal. No more kitchen fires for me for a while. The puppy lay at my feet.

I thought back over the events of the day. The names of my suspects kept running through my mind.

Tears welled in my eyes. Defeat consumed me at the thought I didn't possess the ability to find a killer. Then a new thought hit me. God already knew who murdered Addie! He wanted the killer found and punished. That piece of information was more valuable than any other.

"Oh, God," I prayed aloud, "I can't do this alone. I just turn this whole mess over to You. I ask for guidance to pursue the answers to all my questions. I ask for Your Spirit to invade my heart and give me the discernment to recognize the truth. Help me to put aside my preconceived notions about who is guilty and open my eyes to reality. Thank You, Father, for already beginning to answer my prayer. Amen."

A great peace flooded through me. God was going to show me who killed Addie. I was as sure of it as I had ever been of anything in my entire life.

I swung my feet to the floor and searched for the scuffs I'd discarded when I sat down. I discovered the left one—in Astro's mouth. His jaws worked silently as he chewed on the soft leather. He looked up and tilted his head as if asking what was the matter. I pulled the shoe from his mouth, and he licked at my hand. At that moment, I knew I was hopelessly in love with this little dog.

I laughed and scooped him up. "Well, Astro, I guess you've made yourself right at home. I expect you've seen the last of the kennels. From now on it's going to be the life of a house dog for you."

He answered with a bark and a shake of his head,

almost as if he understood every word I'd said. I hugged him tighter.

"Well, boy, we'd better take you outside, and then we're gonna bed down for the night. Until I'm sure you're housebroken, it's the pet crate for you. After that, who knows? You may even get your own bedroom."

Later when we had both settled down, me in my bed and Astro in his crate next to me, I lay awake and thought how thankful I was for Addie. She taught me so much in the years I lived with her, and even after death she still influenced my life. Who would have ever thought I would have a dog next to my bed?

Hours later something jolted me from a sound sleep, and I sat up. I blinked and peered around the darkened room, but I couldn't figure out what had caused me to awaken. Then I heard it—the dogs barking at the kennels.

"Oh no, it's gonna be another one of those nights."

My feet touched the floor, groping for my slippers, but as usual they weren't where I wanted them to be. My toe caught the side of the pet crate, sending a shooting pain up my leg. The puppy growled, and I bent over and placed my hand over the front of the container.

"Sorry, boy. It looks like your momma and poppa don't want us to get a good night's sleep."

The face of the alarm clock glowed in the dark. One o'clock.

I pushed myself out of bed and groped my way across the room to the window. Maybe if I called out to them they'd settle down. With a grumble, I pulled the curtains aside and looked out toward the kennel.

The security light at the corner of the kennel cast its beams across the kennel. Thick darkness enveloped everything else. We who lived in this area often spoke of how the night settled in our little valley, the mountains blocking any light from crossing their peaks. My nose pressed to the glass of the pane, and I strained to see if the dogs had gotten into the exercise yard.

Just as I placed my hands on the bottom of the window to push it up, I saw movement. I froze in fright at a dark figure leaving the exercise yard and pulling the gate closed. From where I stood, it was impossible to make out whether it was a man or woman. For just a moment the figure stood out in the beams from the security light, and then disappeared in the darkness.

The curtains dropped from my grasp. What had I seen? Whatever it was, I wasn't about to ignore it.

I grabbed the phone and dialed 911. The dispatcher assured me a patrol car was in my area and would arrive within minutes.

I pulled on my robe and went downstairs to wait. Before I knew it, a cruiser was pulling up in front of my house, and two policemen were standing in my entry.

The younger of the two tipped his hat. "You have a prowler, ma'am?"

"Yes. I saw someone down by the kennel."

He smiled. "Now don't you worry. We'll have a look around. If there's anyone here, we'll find him."

They walked out, got flashlights from their car, and headed around the house. I waited for the next twenty minutes for them to return. At last they stepped up on the porch.

"We've checked all the outbuildings and the kennel, and we didn't find anybody. But the lock on the gate into the kennel is broken. Was it broken before tonight?"

Fear bubbled up in me. "No. In fact the man who's taking care of the dogs just fixed it a few days ago."

The policemen exchanged glances. "Do you want to check to see if anything's missing?"

The thought of that figure leaving the exercise area made me shiver. I didn't want to go down there at night, even with a police escort. "Only if I have to." The younger officer smiled. "It's mighty dark down there, and you might not be able to tell anyway. In the morning check it out and let us know."

"I will, and thank you for coming."

"That's what we're here for. And if you have any more trouble tonight, give us a call."

I thanked the two and watched through the front window as they drove away. There was nothing left to do but return to bed.

Convinced I'd never be able to go back to sleep, I crawled into bed, wide-awake now to wait for the dawn. The next thing I knew the shrill ring of the phone on the table jerked me into a sitting position.

The red numbers on the clock blinked 3:04 a.m.

My elbow caught the corner of the lampshade as I reached for the phone, and I grabbed at it with both hands as it tumbled toward the floor. With the light steadied, I swung my legs over the side of the bed before I remembered the dog crate next to it. Same old story—I never learn from my mistakes. I reached down to rub my foot.

The phone jingled again. "Hello," I finally managed.

"Miss Dennison?" a strange voice said.

"Yes, who is this?"

"Sorry to wake you at this hour of the morning."

"That's okay. Who is this?"

"The St. Claire Fire Department. We're calling to inform you that your antique shop is on fire."

"What?" I screamed, fully awake now.

"Yes, ma'am. The call came in five minutes ago, and we've dispatched our trucks to the blaze. You might want to come as quickly as possible."

"I'll be there right away."

I slammed the phone back in its cradle, reached for my jeans and shirt, which lay on the chair in the bedroom, and jerked them on. As I headed for the door, my knees grew weak, and I clutched the wall to keep from falling. All my beautiful antiques.

Marcie. I've got to call Marcie.

I walked back to the phone, picked it up, and punched in her number.

It rang several times before a sleepy voice answered. "Hello."

"Marcie, this is Leigh. I just got a call that the antique shop is on fire. Can you meet me there? I think I'm going to need a friend."

"Oh no. I'll get over there right now."

I struggled to keep from crying. "Thanks. I'm leaving now. I'll see you there."

"Drive carefully," she said before the phone went dead.

I rushed down the stairs, grabbed the keys to Addie's truck, and ran out to where I had left it parked. Barks rose from the direction of the kennel as I sped down the driveway and toward the road. I would have to check on the dogs later. At the moment all I could think about was how Addie gave me money to start my business and how proud she was the day I sold my first piece. With a sinking feeling, I realized the shop probably would be gone before morning dawned.

12

The drive into town seemed longer than usual. The headlights on the truck cut a swath through the thick darkness, but a distant glow lit up the sky and became brighter the closer I got to St. Claire. At the town limits, thick smoke poured into the air, the acrid smell evident even inside the truck.

Emergency vehicles blocked the entrance to the street a block from the shop where the truck screeched to a halt. Bystanders lined the street, their curiosity bringing them out in the wee hours of the morning to watch a fire. The crowd parted as I pushed past them and the police toward the raging blaze that leaped from my store into the air.

Marcie stood across the street from the action. She turned toward me, sorrow written on her face. "Oh, Leigh, I'm so sorry."

The flames shot skyward, my trance-like gaze following them. The hard hours I had worked to make the business successful and the money I invested evaporated into thin air before my very eyes. The loss crushed down on me.

Through tear-blurred eyes I gazed at Marcie. "I can't believe it's all gone."

"But you're insured? Right?"

"Yes. I'll get money, but I can't replace those one-of-a-kind pieces of history." I remembered Marcie's comment about having to use my beautiful antiques for firewood if we couldn't pay the electric bill, and tears spilled from my eyes. My beautiful Queen Anne table was going up in smoke. I couldn't look away from the leaping flames. "Are you sure you blew out all the candles before you left?"

"Yes." She grasped my hand. "I checked every one of them. I remember it perfectly because I wanted to get out new ones for tomorrow in case any were about used up. I took the ones that I thought we needed to discard back to the workroom and then rechecked the ones I'd left out." A little sob sounded in her throat. "Leigh, I know they were all out."

"Is there anything else you can think of that might have started this?"

"Nothing. I turned off all the lights and made sure the coffeepot was unplugged before I left."

I sighed. "It may have been something in the wiring. We'll have to wait for information from the fire department."

Above the noise of the fire trucks, the water from the hose, and the men's shouting, the sound of running footsteps caught my attention. Blake dashed toward us, his frightened face lit by the fire.

He stopped beside us. "What happened?"

"I don't know. I just got a call that my shop was on fire."

He took a step forward. The next instant his arms encircled me, and he whispered words of comfort in my ear.

"I'm so sorry," he said.

Confusion nagged at me, and I pulled away from him. "How did you know about the fire?"

"The sirens woke me. When I saw all the smoke rising from this way, I decided to come see what was on fire. I never dreamed it was your shop."

A crackling sound split the air. The water from the hose was sending sparks flying upward. We backed away some. I stared at the flames wishing I could awaken from this nightmare. "No one's had a chance to talk to me yet. They'll probably let me know something as soon as they can."

Blake took my hand, and we sat down on the edge of the curb. "It could have been some electrical problem. You'll have to wait until they can inspect the remains."

Fresh tears ran down my face. "Oh, Blake, there's not going to be much left. All my beautiful antiques are gone."

He put his arm around me and drew me closer. I rested my head on his shoulder. "Leigh, you may lose your business, but I'm thankful you weren't inside when the fire started. I couldn't stand it if something happened to you."

The attraction to Blake I'd been trying to hold in check burst its bonds. It felt right for him to be here. "I'm so glad you're here."

He squeezed my shoulder. "Wouldn't be anywhere else but with you. You've become very special to me in the last few weeks."

Peace washed over me. "I have?"

He smiled. "I thought you probably knew by now."

It was all too much for me—the fire, his unexpected words, my suspicions about him. I sat there unable to speak.

He leaned closer. "I suppose we have some talking to do later."

I wanted to say something, but my tongue wouldn't move. At that moment one of the firemen walked over to us. Thankful for the reprieve from having to respond, I turned my attention to him. His face, visible inside his fire helmet, was covered in perspiration and soot. "I'm Chief Ormandy," he said. "Are you Miss Dennison?"

I stood up and faced him. "Yes. Can you tell me how the fire started?"

He shook his head. "Don't know yet. We'll talk to you when we get everything under control. There are some questions I'll have for you then."

"Okay," I whispered, and watched him walk back toward the men who aimed a hose toward the roof of the building. With a sudden boom, the top of the structure gave way and crashed downward. The collapse echoed inside me as well.

The crowd grew larger by the moment. Several people from church and others I'd known all my life stepped up to tell me how sorry they were. I thanked each one and prayed a prayer of thanksgiving for such wonderful friends. But many of the people standing around I'd never seen. Probably tourists in town on vacation.

As my gaze flitted across those assembled, my breath caught in my throat. One face snagged my attention among all those present. In the light from the flames, Perry Witherington stood on the fringe of the group, staring at the leaping tongues of fire. I closed my eyes for a moment, and when I opened them again, he was gone. I scanned the crowd, but he was nowhere to be seen.

With a sigh I focused on the men who were fighting to save my property. We sat there for hours watching the firemen as they struggled to get the blaze under control. Just as the first light of dawn streaked across the sky, they at last had some success. The flames disappeared even though the air hung heavy with the smell of smoke.

When it finally appeared that the fire was out and cool enough for some scrutiny, the men began to inspect the various areas that were left. The charred remains stood in stark contrast to the building full of beautiful antiques that it had once been.

Chief Ormandy and his men talked and pointed as they walked around the hollow shell that had once been my antique shop. They disappeared from view for a while before they came around the other side of the building. The men seemed intent on what the chief was saying.

After several moments, Chief Ormandy walked toward us. My muscles groaned in protest as I rose from the curb where we had sat for hours. "Do you know how the fire started?"

He stopped in front of us and shook his head. "Don't know anything for sure yet, but we have our suspicions."

I pressed my hand to my heart. "Suspicions?"

The intensity of his stare sent a warning signal to me. "Have you had problems with anyone lately? Maybe somebody that threatened you."

I thought of the names of the suspects on my legal pad at home. "What makes you ask that?"

Chief Ormandy took off his helmet and wiped his hand across his face. "We've got some red flags about this fire."

Now I was scared. "What kind of red flags?"

"Well, I can't be sure until the investigators get through, but I think this fire was deliberately set."

Blake's arm encircled my shoulders. "What did you find that causes you to think that?" he asked.

"For one thing, the fire had a strange smell to it when we pulled up. And then there was the unusual behavior of the fire. With a building full of furniture and household items you wouldn't expect it to take so long to get it under control."

Blake's arm tightened around me. "Anything else?"

"Yeah. There seems to be several places where the fire originated. That's the mark of arson. It looks like somebody wanted the fire to spread in a hurry, so he piled up debris in places across the back of the shop and lit it. There was even an empty burned can that looks like it might have had some kind of accelerant in it."

"Wouldn't an arsonist be more careful than to

leave a can behind?" Blake asked.

The chief laughed. "You'd think that. But most arsonists leave something behind about 50 percent of the time."

This made no sense. I leaned forward. "But why would anyone want to burn my shop?"

Chief Ormandy rubbed the back of his neck, fatigue showing in his face. "It's hard to tell. Maybe somebody thinks you've wronged them in some way and wants to get revenge."

His words sent a shudder through me. Revenge? Maybe Addie's killer thought I was getting too close and decided to scare me off with a visit to my farm and then to my shop.

The chief looked back at what remained of my shop. "Many arsonists want revenge, and they always target something that's personal to the object of their hate. They want to cause the person to suffer." He shrugged. "Maybe it was random. Who knows? Like I said, we'll know more after the investigators are though. I'll let you know as soon as we have the reports."

We watched as he walked back toward the fire truck that was preparing to leave. He got in, and they pulled out. I was glad to see that one engine with its men stayed behind to monitor the building for a while.

Blake grasped my arms and turned me to face him. "Did you hear what he said, Leigh? Somebody is out to hurt you. This is getting too dangerous. You've got to let the police handle Addie's murder. It's not worth getting yourself hurt—or worse."

I shook my head. "If the murderer did set the fire, then that means I'm getting closer. I can't quit now."

His mouth tightened into a grim line. "Please don't do anything that will put you in further danger."

"I won't."

Marcie stretched her arms above her head and yawned. "Well, we can't do anything else here, I think I'll go on home and get some more sleep."

"I'm tired, too," I said. "I guess I'd better get on home."

Blake grasped my hand. "Why don't we go over to Lou's Diner and have some breakfast? Then I'll go home with you and take care of the dogs."

I didn't want to be alone. "That sounds good. Want to come with us, Marcie?"

She stifled another yawn. "No thanks. I'll come out to the farm later."

I glanced back at the smoldering ruins as Blake and I walked away. My skin tingled with a sudden chill. Somebody had sent me a message tonight.

An hour later I turned the truck into the driveway of the farm. All the way from town I had dreaded returning to the house after the events of the night. The dark figure leaving the kennel still taunted me, and then Perry Witherington showed up at the fire. I didn't know if I would be able to stay at the house alone after the scare it had given me.

The reflection of Blake's truck in the rearview mirror soothed these fears as I pulled to a stop in front of the house. I turned off the engine and sat there thinking about all that had happened since I got home the evening before.

"I'm getting closer, and somebody is worried. But who is it?"

"Leigh," Blake called out. "Are you going to sit in the truck all day?"

With a sigh I opened the door and stepped to the ground. "I guess I was waiting. . ." I turned in the direction of the kennel. "Do you hear that?"

A puzzled expression crossed his face. "What?"

"Nothing!" I cried. "The dogs aren't barking. Hallelujah! Maybe something will go right today after all."

Blake grabbed my hand, and we ran around the house and toward the kennel. Just as we passed the back porch, I stopped, my feet planted on the ground.

"What is it?" Blake asked, a frown pulling his brows downward.

I pointed toward the kennel. "Look."

His gaze followed the direction of my finger, and we stood there staring at the figure of Preacher Cochran coming out of the fenced-in area. He pulled the gate closed just like the person in the moonlight had done the night before. I studied his movements. Did he resemble the figure I had seen, or was it just my imagination?

"Come on, Leigh," Blake urged and pulled me forward.

Preacher turned to face us as we approached. He wore camouflage pants and a T-shirt just as he had the day I caught him in my workshop. His lips were drawn across his teeth in a tight line, and his arms dangled at his side.

"Morning, Preacher," Blake said as we stopped in front of him.

Preacher glanced from Blake to me before he spoke. "Mornin'. Your lock's broke."

Blake stepped around Preacher and groaned. "Oh no. How did this happen?"

"I'll tell you later," I said and turned my attention to Preacher. "What are you doing here?"

He pointed toward the dogs. "They been barkin' all night. I can hear them from where I stay under the bridge. I come over here to see if there was anything I could do for 'em. Miss Addie sure thought a lot of them dogs, and it hurts me to hear 'em carry on so."

I was tempted to ask if he was the one here in the middle of the night. I started to order him off the property but stopped. I had wanted to find a way to keep him around until I found out who the murderer was. Even though he had Addie's Bible, I still wasn't sure if he was the killer, but I had to know.

"You're right, Preacher. Addie did love her dogs. They seem to like it when you're here. Do you think you could drop by from time to time to help with them?"

There, I had said it. My heart pounded.

Blake stepped closer to me. "Leigh, what are you doing?" he whispered.

"You really want me to do that?" Preacher looked at me as if he couldn't believe the words.

"Yes. Ross is coming back to work this morning, and he's gonna need some help. Especially after Blake goes back to school in a few weeks. I don't know anything about taking care of the dogs, but I think Addie taught you a lot."

A grin spread across Preacher's face. "Yes, ma'am, she sure did. I'd like to help Ross again. He's a nice boy."

Blake inched a little closer to me. "We need to talk." He pulled me aside. "Are you out of your mind? You know what we found at the bridge."

Preacher had turned back to the fence and was watching the dogs. "I know," I said. "But I'm going to tell the police about that. Besides Ross will be here to watch him."

I could see indecision on Blake's face. "But still. . ."

I smiled at him. "But you trust Ross, don't you?"

"Well, yes, but—"

"Then everything will be fine. I'm going to need a lot of help if we get Astro ready to show."

"Just be careful." Blake let out a long breath.

"I will." I glanced back at the broken lock and remembered the police officer's words. "By the way, someone broke in here last night. We need to see if anything's missing."

Blake's face blanched. "Somebody broke in *and* your shop burned down? This is getting dangerous."

I stepped closer to Blake and lowered my voice. "I know, and I think it could have been Preacher. We've got to keep an eye on him."

"Don't worry. I will, and I'll warn Ross, too." He stared at me a moment as if he wanted to say more, but he turned and walked back to Preacher. "Let's feed the dogs."

Preacher glanced around at the pen. "Where's the little fella? I couldn't find him."

"Oh no." I gasped. "He's still in the pet crate from last night. I'd better go take him outside right now."

I turned and jogged toward the house, remorseful at how uncomfortable the puppy must be after his long night in the carrier.

"Don't you worry none," Preacher called after me. "We'll take care of everything."

Something about the tone of his voice chilled me. *Take care of everything? That's what I'm afraid of.*

13

The uneasy feeling hadn't left me several hours later as I sat on the back porch and filtered through a mountain of bills, sympathy cards, and advertisements. Astro, tired from his walk and well fed, lay curled up at my feet. "Why didn't you remind me to check the mail?" I said to him. "You know I have trouble remembering minor details." He glanced up at me, yawned, and closed his eyes again. With a laugh I reached down and patted his head. "Well, I can see you're going to be a lot of help."

"There you are." Blake approached the porch. "What're you doing?"

"Going through the mail. It's true what they say about the post office. Neither rain nor sleet nor hail shall stop delivery of the mail."

He sank down in the chair next to me. "That's good to know."

"Yeah. Now if I can just remember the postman's coming and go to the mailbox, I'll be fine."

"I fixed the lock again, and the dogs are all right. Do you want me to check the mailbox before I leave every day?"

"No, I'm going to. . ." I stopped at the lines of fatigue on his face. "Oh, Blake. You look exhausted. You need to go home and get some rest."

My gaze moved over his tired features. I

remembered watching the flames reflected on his face the night before, and I hadn't forgotten the words he'd spoken. He hadn't said anything since, and I was relieved. Even though I recognized my feelings for him, I still had some doubts. And until they were laid to rest, I couldn't run the risk of trusting him fully.

Something soft pushed at my foot, and I glanced down. Astro growled up at me.

Blake laughed. "I think he's jealous of me."

I reached down and picked up Astro. "Sorry, Blake. I guess he wants my undivided attention."

Blake held his hands up in defeat and stood. "Okay. I know when I'm beat. I guess I'll go on home and take a shower." He turned to leave but stopped, a frown on his face. "Ross and Preacher are cleaning the kennels. Do you feel safe staying with them here? I can go home later if you want."

I shook my head. "No, you're tired. Go on and get some rest, then come back later. I'll be fine."

"Are you sure?" He tilted his head, and his eyes narrowed. "I still don't feel good about leaving you here with Preacher."

"Go on." I hugged the puppy tighter. "Ross is here, and besides I've got a great watchdog. We'll be fine."

He studied me for a moment. "How about if I come back later and take you out to eat since we didn't get to go last night?"

"I'd like that."

"Well, see you later. In fact I don't think I'll be able to stay away too long."

With that he stepped off the porch leaving me sitting at the table wondering what in the world I was going to do. I had to solve this murder soon, or I was going to go crazy trying to push Blake away. The bills could wait, but something else couldn't. I had to go to the police.

—

Thirty minutes later I sat facing Detective John Sawyer in his office. All the way into town I had rehearsed what I was going to say. Now that I was here, my prepared speech had vanished from my mind.

He cleared his throat and spread some papers on the desk in front of him. "I was really sorry to hear about your shop burning."

"Thank you."

"I suppose you're here to see if we have any suspects."

I frowned. "Suspects?"

"In the arson. We've just opened an active investigation to find whoever set that fire."

Although I was concerned about the shop, that wasn't my chief reason for being there. "Thank you, but that's not really why I came today."

"Oh?" A look of surprise crossed his face. "Then what can I do for you, Miss Dennison?" He leaned back in his chair and fixed an unwavering gaze on me.

I searched for the words I wanted to say, but they were gone. I swallowed. "Well, Marcie thought I needed to talk to you."

His eyes flickered for a moment, and a smile

creased his face before he recovered, his professional appearance taking over. "And what did Miss Payton want you to tell me?"

"She said you're a really nice person."

Now he did smile. "I'm glad to hear that."

I scooted to the edge of my chair. "But I am, too, Detective Sawyer, and I didn't kill Addie."

He tilted his head. "Go on."

"I've been trying to find out who killed her, but I'm beginning to doubt that I ever will. So I think you need to know some things I've discovered."

Now I had his full attention. "And what's that?"

For the next few minutes, I told him about my list of suspects, the check, Addie's Bible, Celeste and Perry wanting the dogs, and Blake's time alone on the porch, his need for money, and his knowing about the shop vac in my workroom.

He scribbled in his notebook. When I'd finished, he looked up. "Do you have the check you found?"

I pulled it from my purse. "Here it is."

He reached in his desk for a plastic bag, and I dropped the check inside. "Thanks for letting me know all this. You can be assured we'll look into it."

I knew he expected me to leave, and I stood. "Thank you for seeing me, Detective Sawyer. I pray that you'll find out who killed Addie. No matter what you think of me, I loved her like a mother, and I would never have done anything to hurt her."

He got up from his desk and went to open the door for me. As I walked by, he smiled. "From listening to you, you seem to feel guilty that you suspect Blake Cameron. Is that right?"

I bit my lip and looked down at my feet.

He cleared his throat. "Well, you did say he's been helping you a lot at the kennel which would give him access to all areas. If I remember correctly, your workshop is in a building right next to the kennel. Is that right?"

I nodded.

"Hmm, interesting, isn't it? I imagine he's in and out of those buildings all the time."

"I suppose so."

He scrubbed his hand over his jaw as if in deep thought. "It's quite a distance from the house to the kennel, too." He smiled down at me. "You might want to go back and check your timeline of the night of the murder."

What was he inferring? That I might be wrong in suspecting Blake?

"I'll do that," I said. I stepped outside the door and glanced back at him. "And Marcie's right. You are a nice person."

He smiled. "Thanks. For an armchair detective, you are, too."

___

All the way home I thought about what Detective Sawyer had said. He was right. Blake had the keys to the kennel, and my workshop key was on the ring. He could have gone in there anytime over the past few weeks while he was working there. And then it hit me. I struck the steering wheel with my palm. "Why didn't I remember?" When Blake fixed the latch on the gate the first time, he would have gotten the tools from my workshop. He could have seen the shop vac when he was in there.

What a relief. I must have been wrong about him. I jumped to a conclusion without thinking it through. But there was still the time he spent alone while I was upstairs. There was only one way I could think of to check out Detective Sawyer's suggestion about the timeline.

When I got to the farm, I drove to the kennel and stopped in front of my workshop. I didn't see Ross and Preacher as I unlocked the door, got back in the truck, and drove to the front of the house.

I parked the truck where Blake did when he arrived to take me to dinner. I got out and stood at the spot where he'd been when I went back in the house. With a glance at my watch, I ran as fast as I could around the house and toward my workshop. I strained to widen my stride in an effort to match a man's, and my lungs expanded with the extra effort. Panting for breath, I burst through the door, grabbed a tool, and ran back toward the house. By the time I got to the back door, my legs ached in protest.

I pushed the back door of the house open, hurried toward the study, and entered. I swiped the chisel through the air and dropped it on the floor. Then I hurried back outside and positioned myself where Blake had been when I came back outside.

A glance at my watch told me it had taken five minutes to accomplish my task. I also was out of breath and perspiring heavily. When I'd come outside, Blake had been cool, not a drop of moisture on him.

After catching my breath, I tried my experiment again, this time running to the front door and entering there instead of through the back. It took me five and a half minutes.

My next move was to check the time I'd been gone. I stepped onto the porch and entered the house. I ran up the stairs, just as I had done that day, and into my bedroom. I jerked the drawer out, my cosmetics falling to the floor. I dropped to my knees, scooped them up, and replaced the drawer. Then I pretended to put on lipstick, grabbed an imaginary jacket, and dashed back down the stairs. On the bottom step I paused, as I had done then, and glanced at the study. Then I ran outside.

Three minutes.

"Maybe I ran too fast."

I tried it again and again, trying to increase my time to five minutes. When I finally matched the two times, I had reduced my progress up the stairs to a slow walk.

After my last trip up the stairs and down, I fell into a wicker chair on the porch and thought about my experiment. Probably my efforts wouldn't hold water in a court of law, but it didn't matter to me. I had convinced myself of one thing.

Blake Cameron didn't kill Addie.

———

I must have dozed after all my activity, for an hour later I sat up in the wicker chair and rubbed my eyes. Every muscle in my body screamed from fatigue. Something to relax me was what I needed—like a few hours of hard labor in my woodworking shop.

With a guilty start, I realized I hadn't worked in there since the day Preacher took the mortise chisel from its case. The memory of that tool sticking out of Addie's back still haunted me. Maybe that was the reason for my reluctance to handle those tools again.

Astro had been closed up in his crate in the kitchen since I left for the police station. I went in the house and let him out of his quarters. He bounded around my feet, his tail wagging in welcome. I leaned down and petted him.

"Okay, Astro. How about you and me doing some furniture building for a while?"

He jumped up and barked three shrill yelps. The puppy bounded ahead of me out the back door, looking over his shoulder every few seconds to see if I followed. His frisky nature had returned. How different he seemed since his removal from the kennel with Beau and Belle. I still couldn't understand that.

Ross and Preacher were nowhere to be seen as we approached the kennel. Astro stopped to sniff a blade of grass, and I hurried past him. The closer I came to the kennel the more my apprehension increased at allowing the two men to come back to work. Maybe I shouldn't have been so quick to let Blake go home, but he looked dog tired.

I glanced back at Astro who was chasing a butterfly and laughed. "You certainly don't look dog tired. Come on, boy. Let's get in the workshop."

Out of the corner of my eye, I caught a glimpse of Preacher as he stepped outside the kennel to set a broom by the fence. He didn't look my way, and I studied him as he walked back inside the enclosure. Something about the way he moved reminded me of the figure I saw the night before. It was impossible to be certain for there was just a moment's glimpse.

But what if Preacher was the one? I imagined the headlines from the *St. Claire Post*—LOCAL KENNEL OWNER MISSING—and the accompanying story of my mysterious disappearance. *In an effort to find the young woman, a favorite of residents in the area, rescue teams spent days searching the surrounding mountains. With deep regret Detective John Sawyer announced that Leigh Dennison, noted criminal investigator, had disappeared from the face of the earth just like Jimmy Hoffa.*

"You okay?" Preacher's voice brought me plummeting back to reality.

"Uh, yeah. Just lost in thought." I eased toward the woodworking shop.

"Need anything?"

"N—no th—thanks."

With a sigh of relief, I closed the door behind me and leaned against it. My imagination was going to get me in trouble if I didn't watch out. I just had to be careful and watch Ross and Preacher for any sign of trouble.

My last unfinished piece of furniture, a round scalloped tabletop, stood in the center of the room. Astro sniffed around its legs and then hurried across the room, investigating every corner. When he seemed to find the right spot, he settled on the floor and lowered his head onto his front paws.

"Make yourself at home, sir." A small bowl sat on the shelf above my work area, and I poured water into it from the bottle I carried. "There you go, fellow. In case you get thirsty."

Hard work soon made me forget the fears that occupied my thoughts. For the next hour I worked to sand the wood to the right degree of perfection and found myself actually enjoying it. I was so engrossed in my task that I didn't hear anyone at the door.

The puppy jumped to his feet, a soft growl rumbling in his throat.

"Who is it?" I called.

"It's Ross, Miss Dennison. Can I see you for a minute?"

Astro's tail wagged as he ran toward the door. "Stay here," I said, opening the door and wedging through it to the outside.

I pulled the door closed and faced Ross. "What is it?"

"Preacher's already left for the day, and I need to

get home and check on my mother. I'll be back in the morning."

"Fine, Ross. I'll see you then."

He backed up a step and glanced at the door to the workshop. "Mr. Cameron said you were taking care of the puppy today. You know I haven't worked with him since the day I left to go to Cherokee. Do you want me to start his training tomorrow?"

"I think we might do that. We'll talk about it in the morning." I turned to reenter the shop, but I realized Ross hadn't moved. "Is there something else?"

He swallowed and inched closer. "I need to apologize."

I looked for a hint of pretense in his face, but I only saw sincerity. "For what?"

"I talked awful to you that day I got back from Cherokee. I shouldn't have done that. I've tried to tell myself I was upset over Miss Addie's death and my mother's illness. But I know that's not an excuse. I just wanted you to know how sorry I am about that."

"Thank you for telling me, Ross. Apology accepted." He smiled and backed away. "Thanks for letting me come back, Miss Dennison. You won't be sorry."

He walked to the old truck I first saw in his driveway. After several attempts it started, and Ross drove away.

A shrill bark sounded from inside the workshop. "Astro! I forgot all about him."

Astro stood in the middle of the room, a spreading puddle at his feet. With a groan I rushed inside, closing the door behind me. I searched for something to clean up the mess.

After everything was once again in order, I picked up the puppy who licked at my face. "Sorry, boy. It was my fault. I have to remember that you can't tell me when you need to go. I'll have to take you outside more often."

The puppy squirmed, and I held him tighter as I looked around the workshop to make sure everything was in place. A glance at my watch reminded me the afternoon was fading. "We'd better hurry if I'm going to be ready when Blake gets back."

I jerked the door open intending to step outside but instead took a step backward. Preacher Cochran blocked the doorway, his body straight and tall and his arms pressed close to his chest. I backed away slowly, absolute terror consuming me as he advanced. The muscles in his jaw twitched, and his fingers caressed the object he held in his hands—Addie's Bible.

14

I—I thought you'd le–left." I clamped my teeth together to keep them from chattering. Preacher's eyes narrowed as he glanced in the direction of the closed cabinet that housed my tools. The image of the mortise chisel in his hand flashed into my mind.

My foot struck the bowl of water I poured for Astro. The container tipped, and the cold liquid poured across the top of my tennis shoes. I backed farther away. A little water was the least of my worries now.

Preacher advanced toward me. My gaze darted to the door in an effort to gauge my chances of pushing past him. His broad shoulders framed the opening. There was no way around him.

He looked down at Astro squirming in my arms. "He wants down. Why don't you let him go?"

"Of course." I leaned over and deposited Astro on the floor at my feet.

The hinges of the door creaked, and I realized he was pushing it closed. My stomach churned. *I'm going to throw up*, I thought. I swallowed hard and slowly straightened. Preacher stood a few feet away looking down at the puppy. He glanced over his shoulder at the closed door. "I didn't want him to get out."

And you don't intend for me to leave either, I thought. My mind raced to find an escape from the man blocking my way, but it appeared impossible.

Suddenly some long ago advice from my high school basketball coach popped into my mind. Sometimes the best defense is a good offense.

Maybe that was the answer. I held up my arm and looked at my wristwatch. "Blake will be here any minute to pick me up, so tell me what you want."

Preacher's mouth drooped on one side, and his shoulders slumped a little. "I still can't figure out what I done to make you not like me. I thought maybe you'd gotten a little nicer since Miss Addie's death, but I guess not."

I didn't answer him. We stood there facing each other, neither moving for a moment. It reminded me of how children stare at each other, daring the other to look away. After a moment, he let out a long breath and held out Addie's Bible.

He pushed the leather volume toward me. "Here. I think it's fittin' that you have her Bible. So I brung this over to give to you."

I could almost feel the hairs bristling on my arms. "Wh–what?"

He pushed the book into my hands. "I think she'd want you to have this now. She sure did love you. Talked about you all the time, almost as much as she did her son."

The smooth cover of the Bible felt warm in my hands. "How did you get this?"

He bit down on his lip then answered. "She gave it to me."

That couldn't be true. "Come on now. You don't

expect me to believe that she gave you her most prized possession—the last gift from her son."

"I know it's hard to believe, but it's true. It happened the day she got killed."

"What happened?"

Preacher stared off into space for a moment before he started speaking. "I felt real bad that I came into your workshop. I didn't mean to hurt your tools none. I just wanted to look at 'em. Me and my dad used to build things when I was a boy. Seein' your shop brought back a lot of memories for me."

He reached in his pocket, pulled out a bandana, and wiped his nose. "When you run me off, I went back to the bridge. I decided I'd done stayed too long here, so about an hour later I come back over here to tell Miss Addie good-bye. She'd been mighty good to me, and I couldn't just up and leave without telling her."

"An hour? I was still there at that time."

"Yeah, she said you was gettin' ready to go out, but she wanted to get you back downstairs to let me explain why I was in your shop. I told her no, 'cause I knew you'd never believe me."

"What did she say?"

"She was sittin' at her desk, and I was standin' in front of it. She kinda folded her hands on top of it and sat there a couple a seconds with her eyes closed. When she opened 'em, there was tears in her eyes. She reached over to the side of the desk and picked up her Bible and held it kinda like she was strugglin' with somethin'."

I could hardly contain my interest at this point. "What did she do next?"

He blinked as if to stop the tears I could see in his eyes. "She came around that desk and held out her Bible to me. I'll never forget how she looked standin' there. It was like God was right next to her as she gave it to me. Then she said, 'Preacher, my son gave me this Bible when he went to Vietnam. He didn't get to come home, but you did. If he'd ended up wanderin' around the country like you, I'd hope somebody would have told him that Jesus loves him more than anything.' "

I was crying now, for I knew the words he spoke sounded so much like Addie.

"She said, 'Vietnam took my son and left a big hole in my heart. It took you away from your family and everything you loved. Vietnam doesn't need to claim any more victims. Let's stop it right here today. You take my Bible and find out how much God loves you.' "

"And you took it?"

"Yeah," he murmured. "I tried not to, but she wouldn't have it no other way. She said, 'If you don't start tryin' to understand how God can heal your hurt, you're gonna be running from people who don't understand you for the rest of your life.' "

"Was she talking about me?"

He nodded. "I think maybe she was. And I found out how right she was about God lovin' me. I read it in her Bible." He took a deep breath. "So I decided maybe you needed to keep it more than I do. Maybe I'm not the only one who don't understand how God can love someone like me."

I pressed the Bible to my chest to keep from dropping it. "Thank you, Preacher," I whispered.

"No, ma'am. Thank you for lettin' me come back to work here. I sure do love Miss Addie's dogs."

He turned, walked to the door, and opened it. Before he stepped outside, he turned. "I'll be back in the mornin' if'n you still want me."

"Yes, I do." And I meant it from my heart. "I'll see you in the morning."

He smiled and disappeared out the door. I stood in the middle of the shop wondering what to do next. The puppy nuzzled at my feet. I dropped to my knees, picked him up, and held him and the Bible next to my body.

In that moment, I could feel God's presence in the room, and I raised my voice to Him. "Oh, God, help me to be more like Addie."

I stayed on my knees for several moments, and then I arose. My heart felt full, and I knew peace from the Holy Spirit filled me. The murder still remained unsolved, but I had come to one conclusion—Preacher Cochran did not kill Addie.

I pulled my cell phone from my pocket and pushed the number I'd programmed in after seeing the prowler at the kennel.

A young woman's voice answered. "St. Claire Police Department."

"This is Leigh Dennison. I need to speak to Detective Sawyer."

Within seconds he answered. "This is John Sawyer. How can I help you?"

"Detective Sawyer, some things have happened since I left your office this afternoon that have led me to believe that neither Blake Cameron nor Preacher Cochran had anything to do with Addie's death. Do you have time for me to tell you?"

At dinner that night, I told Blake about going to see the police and then about what Preacher had told me. I left out the part about suspecting Blake.

Later, on the way home, Blake brought up the subject again. "I'm glad you went to see Detective Sawyer. You did the right thing."

"Um, I guess so." I thought about what Marcie had said about the policeman and how interested he seemed when I mentioned her name. "You know what? I think that detective and Marcie are attracted to each other."

Blake glanced at me. "Are you all right with that?"

I sat silent for a moment. "I suppose I am. I just keep thinking of the things he said to me the night of the murder. He acted like I was the one who was guilty."

"He was only doing his job, Leigh. You should be glad he took it so seriously. You wouldn't have liked it if he'd seem disinterested in the case."

I sighed. "I suppose you're right. And I do want Marcie to be happy. She deserves someone special. I just hope John Sawyer realizes what a wonderful person she is."

"I'm sure he does."

The truck rattled over the bridge, and I peered into the dark. Preacher was nowhere to be seen.

As we rounded the curve in the driveway, the house came into view. Light streamed from every window. Ever since I'd moved back home, I made sure lights were on in every room in the evenings. Maybe before long I would feel safe enough to come home to an unlit house at night.

We stopped, and dread built up in me at having to enter alone. Almost as if he read my mind, Blake spoke. "Want me to go inside with you for a few minutes?"

I shook my head. "No need for that. I set the alarm system before I left."

We got out of the truck and walked hand-in-hand up the front steps and onto the porch.

"I had a wonderful time tonight. I wish we could do it again tomorrow, but I can't."

My eyebrows arched. "Why not? Are you working at the school again?"

"No. I have to go to Charlotte."

I felt guilty because I hadn't asked Blake about his father. "How's your dad?"

"My mother called again today, and she's really worried about him. I need to go for a few days and check on him."

"I'm sorry I haven't asked you about him lately."

"No problem. I really thought he was doing better. Especially since he'd taken care of his financial worries."

"I remember you telling me that your parents found the money to pay their medical bills."

"Yeah. Dad finally sold some property. It'd been on the market for months, and he'd about given up on ever selling it."

I hoped my face didn't reveal the remorse I felt over the doubts I'd harbored about Blake. I took his hand in mine and met his gaze. "I know what it's like to lose a parent, Blake. You go help your mother and treasure every minute you can spend with them."

A mist covered his eyes. "I will, Leigh."

The thought of going for even one day without seeing Blake made me want to cry. Putting on the bravest front I could, I smiled. "I'll miss you."

He stared at me for a moment. "I'll miss you, too. These past few weeks have been wonderful for me. I hope it's been the same for you." He started to say something, seemed to change his mind and smiled. "I want you to be careful while I'm away." He put his finger under my chin and lifted my face. "I don't want to leave you until the murderer is caught, but I need to check on my father."

"I understand. Don't worry about me."

"And call the police at any hint of trouble. Okay?"

"I promise. I will."

He squeezed my hand. "I'll be back in three days. You take care of yourself."

As he backed toward the porch steps, a thought struck me. "Blake, what about Red? Is he going with you?"

He stopped and walked back toward me. "I thought I would take him. But to tell you the truth, my mother doesn't like him very much. So maybe a kennel."

"No, let him stay with me while you're gone. Astro and I would love the company."

He hesitated. "Are you sure?"

"Yes, bring him by here when you leave in the morning."

He smiled. "Okay, if you insist."

I gave him a little shove toward the steps. "Now go on home and get ready for your trip."

After he left, I stepped into the house, closed the door, and leaned against it thinking of how wonderful the world would be right now if only I knew who killed Addie.

From upstairs a bark sounded, jarring me back to reality. "Oops, Astro. I'd better get you out of your crate and take you outside before we have a problem."

I bounded up the stairs as if my feet floated on clouds. Energy surged through my body, and I wondered if I should use it to attack the pile of bills on the desk. I might as well, I thought. I probably wasn't going to sleep all night.

I awoke the next morning from a sound sleep, refreshed and feeling ready for the day. Much to my surprise, the night passed without any barking from the direction of the kennels. Maybe things were about to return to normal.

The morning seemed too beautiful to stay inside. With Astro in tow, I took my coffee and settled myself in the wicker swing on the front porch. Within minutes, Blake drove up in front of the house with Red in the back of his truck.

"Morning, lovely lady." Blake jumped out of the truck and let the tailgate down for Red.

"Good morning, yourself. And the top of the morning to you, sir." I bent down to pat Red who had jumped on the porch in front of the swing.

Blake placed his hand over his heart and stared into the heavens. "It's true. My dog has stolen your affections."

I laughed and walked down the steps to where he stood by the truck. "You have to admit he's a great looking guy."

"Yeah, well, this great looking guy has to go." Blake grinned and jumped back in the truck. "Take care of yourself, and I'll see you in a few days."

"See you." I waved as he drove away.

Red and Astro lay side by side on the porch. I walked back up the steps and stood looking down at them. "You two sure are lazy."

"I'll second that." Preacher stood at the bottom of the steps.

"Good morning, Preacher. You're a little early."

"Thought I'd come on over and get started."

I glanced down at the coffee cup in my hand. "Would you like some coffee?"

Surprise lit his face. "That would be real nice."

I motioned to the swing. "Have a seat, and I'll go get you a cup. Want anything in it?"

"Black's fine."

When I returned with the coffee, Red lay at the far end of the porch in a spot of sunshine, and Preacher sat in the swing, the puppy in his lap. His fingers stroked Astro's back, and the dog lay still.

"He seems contented." I stopped outside the door and studied the two. Red raised his head, sniffed the air, and then settled back down.

"I like the little fella," Preacher said.

"Me, too."

"Morning." Ross James appeared around the corner of the house.

"Ross, I didn't know you were here."

He walked toward us but stopped at the foot of the steps. "Yeah, I drove in about half an hour ago. I just went straight on down to the kennels. Didn't want to bother you. I saw Mr. Cameron leave, but I didn't know Preacher was here."

The warm handles of the coffee cups reminded me to offer him some. "Want coffee, Ross?"

"No, thanks." He climbed the steps onto the front

porch. "I don't drink. . ."

He stopped in mid-sentence, his eyes staring at Preacher still sitting in the swing holding Astro. A frown wrinkled his forehead, and he turned questioning eyes at me.

"I didn't know you had a new puppy. Where did you get him?"

Laughter rumbled in my throat. The coffee sloshed on my hand, and I winced at the hot liquid on my skin. "That's not a new puppy, Ross. That's Astro."

He shook his head, his forehead creased, and his eyebrows drew down in a frown. He pointed to the dog and wagged his finger. "I don't know where this puppy came from, but I do know one thing. That's not Astro."

15

Both of the coffee cups I held tilted forward, their contents spilling out on the porch. My mouth gaped open. "Come on, Ross, this is no time to be kidding me."

He shook his head and walked toward Preacher who looked just as surprised as I was. He leaned down and patted the puppy that peered up at him. His fingers caressed the drooping tips of the ears as if he wanted them to stand straight. After a few attempts, he grunted and ran his hand across the area between the ears as if he was feeling the skull.

He ran his fingers over the body and each of the legs before he opened the dog's mouth and examined his teeth. When he finished, he stepped back and shook his head.

"Nope, that's not Astro."

"But how can you tell? He's a beautiful dog."

Ross continued to study the puppy. "Yeah, he is. He's ideal for a pet, but he doesn't have the body structure that Astro has."

"But Dr. Baker didn't say a word about it when he examined him."

Ross pursed his lips. "But he'd never seen Astro before, had he?"

"Well, no. But you'd think a veterinarian—"

"Oh no," Ross interrupted. "He wouldn't necessarily

be trained to judge the standard of every breed."

I set the coffee cups down on the table between the wicker chairs and faced Ross, thoughts rumbling through my mind like a freight train. "Are you certain this isn't Astro?"

"Yes, for one thing, I can tell just by looking at him. His ears aren't erect like Astro's, and his skull is narrow and flat. It should be broad and slightly rounded with more width between the ears. His teeth are too small, and he doesn't have the scissors bite like Astro."

I swallowed back the coffee I could feel rising in my throat. "Anything else?"

Ross pursed his lips and ran his hands over the dog again. "Well, his eyes are too close together, and his neck is too long."

"You make him sound like he's not a very desirable dog." The need to defend this puppy that had come to mean so much to me in the last few days rose up in me.

"Oh no. He just doesn't come up to the breed standard to do well in the show ring. You remember Miss Addie said very few dogs do. In fact in a litter you may only have one or even none that are born with the qualities to enter the show ring."

I walked over and took the puppy out of Preacher's arms and held him close. A memory popped into my head—Blake scratching the puppy on the neck and the strange feeling I had that something wasn't right. *It was his ears.* They didn't stand up like I remembered on Addie's dog. Why had I not recognized the difference right away? But then neither had Preacher.

"He may not be a show dog, but he's special to me."

Ross reached out and scratched the dog's ears. "He is a cute little thing, but he's definitely not a show dog."

"Well, I don't care if he. . ." I stopped as the truth seeped into my mind. "If this isn't Astro, where is he?"

Ross shrugged. "Beats me."

Preacher stood and took a step closer. "I never could figure out why them dogs seemed so upset all the time. I guess we know now."

I sank down in one of the chairs still clutching the puppy. "This makes no sense. Someone must have switched the puppies. But who would have anything to gain by doing something like that?"

Ross rubbed the back of his neck. "I checked on the dogs right before I left in Miss Addie's truck, and Astro was in the kennel then."

"So whoever switched them came between the time you left and I arrived home." My heart pounded. "Maybe it was the person who killed Addie."

"What?" Ross said.

I jumped up from the chair. "Of course. Why didn't I see it before? Addie wasn't killed for the money in the bank deposit. She was murdered for the puppy. The murderer must have come here intending to switch the dogs, and Addie confronted him. He had to kill her to cover up the switch and didn't think anyone would figure out the puppy in the kennel was an imposter."

"But who would want Astro bad enough to kill to get him?" Ross asked.

Preacher gave a little grunt. "Nobody I can think of but that highfalutin woman that drives that big white SUV."

The memory of silver-lens sunglasses flashed into my mind. "Or her stepson Perry Witherington," I whispered. "Celeste and Perry want some new breeding stock."

But murder? Could they be capable of that? I reached for the arm of the chair.

Ross and Preacher stepped toward me, and they each grasped one of my arms and eased me down into the chair. They stood facing me. I could hardly look at them for the shame I felt at thinking one of them killed Addie. All the time it had been one or both of the Witheringtons. But which one? Only a monster would stab an elderly woman in the back and watch her die.

Ross touched my shoulder. "What are we going to do?"

I rubbed my forehead. "I don't know. If we had some way to prove this is another dog, we'd have something to go to the police with."

Ross, his lips parted in a grin, squatted down beside my chair. "But we *can* prove it!"

I felt defeated to the bone. "But how?"

"I remember Miss Addie telling me that the American Kennel Club has a voluntary program to help breeders identify their registered dogs. When Astro was born, she sent a sample of his DNA to the offices in Raleigh to be kept on file. All we have to do is check this dog's DNA against what's on file there."

I sat up straight. "How do we do that?"

"We have some extra kits down at the kennel. We'll get a sample from this dog and send it to Raleigh. They can compare it and let us know if it matches what they have."

Ross turned and hurried down the steps. Red, who lay at the far end of the porch, barked as Ross disappeared but then settled back in the warm sunlight.

Preacher sat in the swing, and we waited in silence for Ross to return. Within minutes he ran back around the side of the house and bounded onto the front porch. In his hand he held an envelope and a small swab.

He knelt in front of me and wedged the puppy's mouth open. "Okay, boy, this isn't going to hurt a bit."

"Let me help." I held the puppy's jaws apart, and Ross inserted the swab into its mouth. The dog's jaw wiggled as it rubbed the inside of his mouth.

Ross drew the swab out. "There, little guy. We won't bother you anymore."

"What now, Ross?"

He put the sample inside the pre-addressed envelope he'd brought from the kennel and sealed it. "We mail this, and then we wait for the answer. I can run it to the post office if you like."

"Thanks, Ross. I'll call the AKC headquarters in Raleigh and tell them we're sending this overnight mail because we need a rush on this."

Preacher stood up and followed Ross to the edge

of the porch. "I better get back to work."

"Wait." They stopped and turned to face me. I swallowed hard and blinked wondering if I could say what I needed to speak. "Thank you both so much. Addie would be proud of you."

Neither one said a word.

Taking a deep breath, I continued. "I judged both of you by what I saw on the outside instead of looking in your hearts the way Addie did. Maybe the things she tried to tell me are finally taking root."

Ross shoved his hands in his pocket. "She was one-of-a-kind all right. And she sure did love you."

"Thanks, Ross. I'm going to always remember that."

The two men left me standing there, lost in thoughts of happier days. Red stood up from his spot on the front porch, stretched, and followed me to the door. I reached down and caressed his head, and his nose came up to sniff my hand. "Red, I sure do wish Blake were here. In fact let's call him right now."

I pulled out my cell phone and dialed his number. I smiled when I heard his voice.

"Hi, Blake. Where are you?"

"I've just gone through Asheville. Is anything wrong?"

"Well, I do have some news for you."

"What? Are you okay?"

"Yes." I told him about the puppy and the DNA sample. "So I guess we'll wait a few days to find out the results."

"Then you'll let the police handle it?"

"Yes, I promise."

"Good. I don't want—"

"Blake?" I said, but he didn't answer. I supposed he lost my signal. I'd talk to him later.

The puppy stirred in my arms, and I hugged him. "I guess I'm going to have to come up with a new name for you. I'll have to think about that and how I'm going to make it up to Ross and Preacher for thinking one of them was a killer. Too many things are going through my head right now."

A difficult task lay ahead of me if I was to bring a murderer to justice, and I had to concentrate on that. No distractions for me. Now was the time for my mind to focus on what was important. Other things could wait until a killer was behind bars.

❧

Later that afternoon with all the chores completed at the kennel, Ross closed the gate as the three of us stepped outside the fence. The afternoon had flown by as we worked side by side ever since Ross returned from the St. Claire post office. A few weeks ago, I would never have imagined myself enjoying time with Ross and Preacher so much.

The buildings gleamed from the scrubbing Preacher had given them, and the dogs' food and water bowls were full thanks to Ross. He had even used Beau and Belle to show me some of the training techniques that Addie had taught him.

Running a kennel was certainly a lot of work, and one that required a dedicated person to perform the tasks in caring for the animals. Gratitude for all that Blake had done for me since Addie's death filled me. "What a great guy."

Preacher glanced at me. "What'd you say?"

A laugh rippled from my throat. "I'm talking to myself. I do that a lot."

Beside me, Ross chuckled. "I noticed that. You carried on quite a conversation with yourself all afternoon."

My cheeks grew warm. "Really?"

"Just kidding." He glanced at Preacher and winked.

"Well, now you know my secret, guys. My mouth works sometimes without my brain's knowledge."

The three of us laughed, and I wondered why I never liked these two before. Almost as if he could read my thoughts, Ross glanced away and straightened the bill on the cap he wore and adjusted it to his head. For the first time I noticed the logo on it was for the St. Claire High School baseball team.

Ross turned back around at that moment and saw me staring at the cap. His cheeks flushed, and he pulled the bill down farther over his eyes. "I used to play on the team."

"Oh." There was so much about Ross and Preacher I didn't know, but I was determined to find out in the days ahead.

"Did you call them people at the AKC?" Preacher asked.

The question drew me back to the moment. "Yes. They're going to contact me as soon as they know anything."

Ross let out a long breath. "The clerk at the post office assured me that our envelope would arrive tomorrow. So now we just wait." He looked over his shoulder to where his truck sat. "Well, I'd better get going. One of my mother's friends is bringing dinner over to the house for the two of them. I told her I'd let them have the house to themselves. Guess I'll stop by the Dairy Bar and get a hamburger."

He turned and started toward his truck. Preacher followed. "I'll get on back, too. See you in the mornin'."

"Wait." They both stopped and turned to face me. "Blake's out of town, and I don't want to eat alone. Would you like to join me for dinner?"

Their eyes widened, and they looked at each other before turning back to me. Ross tilted his head. "Are you sure?"

"Yes, but don't expect me to cook. Let's all go to the Dairy Bar. My treat for an afternoon of hard work."

Ross smiled. "Sounds good to me."

"Me, too," Preacher added.

"I'll just be a few minutes." I picked up the puppy that had seemed to be underfoot all afternoon and called to Red who lumbered ahead of me.

Preacher's hand touched my arm. "Give me the puppy, and I'll take him and Red for a walk while you're gettin' ready."

Fifteen minutes later, I held the front door open for Red and the puppy to run inside from their romp with Preacher and led them upstairs to my bedroom. The puppy scampered right into his crate where his food and water waited, and Red settled down next to the bowls I'd left for him.

"Now you two behave yourselves until I get back." Closing the bedroom door, I hurried back down the stairs. I opened the front door and was just about to push the screen open but stopped at the sound of a male voice. Perry Witherington stood just a few feet away from me.

"Where is Miss Dennison? I need to see her."

Ross cleared his throat. "She's busy right now. I'll be glad to give her a message, though, if you'd like for her to call you."

"No, I'm going out with friends tonight. I just thought while I was in the area, I'd drop by. Just tell her I was here."

"We'll do that," Ross said.

The urge to peek outside welled up in me, but now was not the time to face him, not until proof arrived from the AKC. His footsteps crunched on the gravel in the driveway, and I could envision him walking back to his car, the silver-coated sunglasses covering his eyes.

"Oh, by the way," Perry said, "how are the dogs doing?"

"They're fine," Ross answered. "Preacher and me are taking good care of them. I expect one of us will be around here with Miss Dennison all the time from now on."

"Really? How nice for her."

The car door slammed, and the engine started. I crept to the window in the room next to the entry hall and pulled the curtain back. Perry climbed into the Escalade where George Daniel waited. The engine cranked, and they drove slowly down the driveway.

As soon as the car disappeared, I moved outside to the porch. Ross and Preacher stared in the direction Perry had driven.

"Thanks for sparing me the pleasure of his company today."

Ross pulled his cap down on his head and smiled. "I didn't think you needed that. Well, are we ready to go?"

"Yes, let me lock the front door, and I'll be ready. Preacher, you can ride with me, and I'll drop you off at the bridge when we come back."

He shook his head. "I don't think so."

"Are you afraid to ride with me because I talk to myself?"

"No. I don't trust them Witheringtons. One of them might come back here in the middle of the night. I 'spect I better curl up here on your front porch tonight."

I sucked in my breath. "I couldn't ask you to do that."

He gave a little laugh. "I've slept under a bridge most nights. This would be a treat. If you could spare me a blanket, I'll make it fine."

Tears filled my eyes. "Thank you, Preacher. I sure would feel safer to know you're here."

He slapped Ross on the back. "Then it's settled. Let's go get somethin' to eat. I'm starved."

I walked down the steps and stood between them, looking from one to the other. "Me, too."

How things changed in one short afternoon. The day before they were my two chief suspects in a murder, and now they seemed like old friends.

I looped my arms through theirs. "This is weird. I feel like a celebrity. I have bodyguards."

The fact that it was Preacher Cochran and Ross James made it even stranger.

16

Three mornings later, I sat in my kitchen having my first cup of coffee for the day. The late July sun streamed through the window. Jimbo, as I had christened the puppy, and Red lay side by side in front of the sink. I smiled at the two and how they seemed to have bonded in the time Blake had been away. How I wished he would come back soon.

My cell phone rang, and I reached for it. "Hello."

"Good morning."

I sat up straight, my heart pounding. "Blake! I didn't expect to hear from you this morning. I thought you'd be on your way home by now."

"That's what I'm calling about. It looks like I'm going to be delayed another day here. I wanted to check on you."

I jumped to my feet and clutched my cell phone tighter. "Is something wrong? Your father's not worse, is he?"

"No, everything seems to be going well for him, but his tests show that he's diabetic. He's going to be on insulin, and he has to change his eating habits. Mom is going to have to learn a new way of cooking."

I breathed a sigh of relief. "Tell your dad to do whatever the doctor says."

Blake gave a little laugh. "I will. My mother has a lot of errands for me today, and I'm not sure what time I'll be finished. So I'll probably just wait until tomorrow morning to come back."

I swallowed back my disappointment and tried to sound cheerful. "Well, you be careful on the drive home."

"Has the AKC contacted you yet?"

"Not yet. I thought they might call yesterday, but they didn't."

"Ever since you called and told me about the dogs, I've been worried about you." His voice cracked as he spoke. "If it turns out the puppy is an imposter, contact the police right away."

"I will, Blake. I just hope no one finds out about this and alerts the Witheringtons. With their connections, they'd probably whisk Astro out of the country and sell him into the dog slavery trafficking in South America, and then I'd never be able to prove who killed Addie."

A chuckle sounded over the line. "Leigh, there is no slavery trade for dogs."

"Well, you know what I mean. They'd get rid of him some way."

"Be careful, Leigh. Don't do anything foolish. Do you understand?" The concern in Blake's voice vibrated over the telephone.

"And Leigh. . ."

"Yes?"

"Do you remember the night of the fire I told you we needed to talk?"

The intensity of his voice made my pulse race and sent tingles down my spine. "I remember," I whispered.

"As soon as I get back, I want to do that."

His words warmed me like nothing I'd ever experienced before. "Okay."

He hesitated a moment. "So tell Ross and Preacher to keep watch until I get back."

The phone felt hot against my cheek. "You don't have to worry. Preacher's slept on the porch for the past two nights, and Ross is here during the day."

"I'm glad they're watching over you. Tell them to stay close until I get back."

"I will."

"Well, I hope to see you tomorrow." He cleared his throat and then spoke in almost a whisper. "I've missed you, Leigh."

My throat constricted and threatened to choke off my words. "I've missed you, too," I finally managed to say. "Now don't worry. We're fine here. Have a good visit with your folks, and I'll see you tomorrow."

Jimbo and Red raised their heads as I hung up the phone. A tear stood in the corner of my eye, and I brushed at it. "It's still hard to believe, but I can tell that Blake Cameron is interested in me."

The dogs tilted their heads, their expressions looking almost skeptical. "Oh, it's true. He told me I've become special to him. I suppose that means ADD and all." I knelt beside Red and scratched him behind the ear. Jealous of the attention, Jimbo nudged my fingers with his wet snout. I laughed and scratched him, too, a thought from my teenage years flashing into my mind. "Of course I haven't told him my high school senior class voted me the girl most likely to disappear into the jungles of the Amazon while trying to find my way home from the supermarket."

Both dogs growled, and I laughed. "I guess that was the first time I realized my inability to concentrate for very long was obvious to everybody around me."

With a sigh, I stood up. A box of dog biscuits sat on the counter next to the sink, and I grabbed some and shoved them into my jeans pocket for Red and Jimbo to have later. "It's nice to have you guys to talk with, but there's a lot of work to be done today. We might as well get started."

The dogs jumped up just as the phone jingled. Maybe this was the call I'd been waiting for. "Hello."

"This is the AKC offices in Raleigh calling for Miss Leigh Dennison," a voice on the other end of the line said.

I pulled a chair from the table and sank down in it. "I'm Leigh Dennison."

"You asked us to call you as soon as we had an answer to your query about the DNA sample you submitted. I'm putting the results in the mail to you this morning, but since you were so eager to receive the answer, I'm calling to tell you first."

"Thank you." My heart started pounding, and I squeezed the receiver.

"Our lab has done a thorough check of the sample you sent. It doesn't match the one registered by Mrs. Addie Jordan six months ago."

My breath came in little puffs now. "Are you certain?"

"Oh yes. DNA identification is a very exact science."

"Is there any way to identify the dog with this DNA?"

"I'm sorry, Miss Dennison. Profiling is voluntary for kennel owners, and we have no record of ever receiving this dog's DNA."

Of course not. The Witheringtons wouldn't leave a trail that could trace the puppy in my possession back to them. I'd have to find the answer some other way.

"Thank you so much. You've helped me tremendously."

"I'm putting the written report in our outgoing mail right now. You should have it in a few days."

"Thank you again."

I stood up and dropped the phone on the table. Why hadn't I seen it all along? Celeste and Perry Witherington had been so insistent on buying the puppy. One of them undoubtedly switched the two dogs. If they had regained possession of Jimbo, I never would have been able to prove there had been an imposter that prompted Addie's death.

The blood pounding in my ears rose to dangerous levels as I fought the urge to charge over to Celeste Witherington's kennel and demand to see her dogs. Common sense took over, however, and I knew there was only one thing to do.

The number at the police department was becoming all too familiar. I picked up my phone and punched the speed dial. The call was answered by the same woman I'd talked to before. She connected me with Detective Sawyer right away.

I could almost hear a sigh of resignation when he answered. "And what is it now, Miss Dennison?"

"I need you to come out to my kennel. There's something important I have to tell you. I think this will help you find Addie's killer."

"I was just leaving on another matter, but if you think this is urgent, I can stop by."

"Oh, it is. I've discovered the motive for Addie's murder."

There was a moment of hesitation before he responded. "Is that so? In that case I'll be right there."

I hung up and headed out the back door, Red and Jimbo on my heels. Fury built in me as I stormed across the yard toward the kennels. How dare that woman and her weasel of a stepson come over here and pretend sympathy over Addie's death when one of them had killed her. Well, they weren't going to get away with it. Not if I had anything to do with it.

The gate to the exercise area swung wide with the shove I gave it. "Ross, Preacher? Where are you?"

They ran from inside the building, Ross leading the way. "What's the matter?"

"I just got a call from the AKC offices. You were right. The DNA doesn't match."

Ross took his cap off and rubbed his arm across his forehead. "We knew this was going to be the answer we got. Now we can go to the police."

"I've just called them. They should be here in a few minutes."

"Good," Preacher said. "Now maybe we can git to

the bottom of Miss Addie's murder."

Ross tugged on the bill of his cap. "What are you gonna tell them when they get here?"

"I'll tell them you knew Jimbo was not Astro and about the sample we sent to AKC headquarters." A sudden thought struck me. "Do we have any more of those kits?"

"Yes, ma'am. Do you need another one?"

"I think the police will need it when they find Astro at Celeste's kennel."

Ross turned and ran back to the building. Preacher took a step closer and peered at me with serious eyes. "What if they don't find Astro, Miss Dennison? What we gonna do then?"

I had not even considered the possibility of Astro not being at Celeste's kennel. I sucked in my breath and pressed my hands tightly together. "I don't know, Preacher. I suppose we'll just have to find another way to prove she stole Astro."

The smile I leveled at him seemed to satisfy him. He wouldn't have been so accepting of my assurances if he'd known the turmoil I felt inside. I had no idea what I'd do if Astro wasn't at Celeste's kennel.

Ross, Preacher, and I waited outside the kennel exercise area for the arrival of Detective Sawyer. Even though I glanced at my watch every few minutes, I fought the urge to pace up and down beside the fence. Jimbo chased every butterfly he saw and explored every blade of grass in the yard, but Red seemed content lying at my feet.

Red lifted his head and barked when the police car entered the gravel drive that led from the house to the kennel. I leaned down and patted him. "It's okay, fella."

His big eyes watched the progress of the car. Red pushed to his feet as Detective Sawyer got out and moved to stand in front of me. I glanced down at the big dog and smiled. It was evident to me he was positioning himself to protect me if needed.

I stroked his back and leaned over to whisper to him. "Steady, boy."

Red's protective stance wasn't lost on Detective Sawyer. "It seems you have a bodyguard, Miss Dennison." He glanced at Preacher and Ross before he looked back at me. "Now what is it you have to tell me?"

As soon as I started talking, he pulled the familiar notepad from his pocket and began to write in it. How I wished I could grab that pad and read everything he'd written since I first met him. Instead, I told him about the DNA sample and my suspicion that Celeste had switched the puppies.

"And so," I concluded, "I want you to get a search warrant and go to Celeste's kennel. I'm sure you'll find Astro there. Then you'll have Addie's murderer."

Detective Sawyer pursed his lips, frowning before he responded. "Miss Dennison, the police can't go in and search someone's home or business without strong evidence. If we entered the home of everyone we suspect, we could end up depriving everybody of their right to privacy." My face must have mirrored the despair I felt inside for he stared at me for a moment, then he glanced at Ross and Preacher who also looked upset. He cleared his throat. "Tell you what. I'll call the sheriff over at Macon Falls and get them to go to Celeste's house. He can request permission to look around. If she grants it, then he can see if he finds anything out of the ordinary. We call that a knock-and-talk."

"But Celeste won't let them look if Astro's there." My voice sounded strange to my ears as I struggled to suppress tears.

"I'm sorry, Leigh. But it's the best I can do."

I wanted to scream at him that his best wasn't good enough. If Celeste refused to let them search the kennel, she could hide Astro somewhere else. Then I'd never know for sure who killed Addie. I bit my lip and brushed at my eyes. "When will you call?"

He pulled a cell phone from his pocket. "I'll get in touch with our dispatcher right away and have the chief do it. We should know something by the end of the afternoon."

"Let me give you my cell phone number so you can call when you know anything."

He programmed the number into his phone as I recited it. "I'll call as soon as I know anything."

"Thank you, Detective Sawyer. I have a feeling, though, I won't be getting good news."

He frowned. "Now that's not entirely true. You've

given us a great lead. If the police can't get inside the kennel, you can be assured they'll keep a close watch on Celeste. If she's guilty, she'll make a wrong move, and they'll be ready."

This was the most encouraging news I'd had. "Do you really think so?"

"Yes." He smiled. "And one more thing, I want to congratulate you on giving us this piece of information. Now we believe the murder is related to the puppy's disappearance, so we have a new direction. I believe you're smarter than the average armchair detective. Good work, Miss Dennison."

I glanced at Ross and Preacher who beamed their approval. "Why, thank you, Detective Sawyer."

"You're welcome. Now if you'll excuse me, I have a phone call to make."

He punched a number in the phone and headed back to the car. As he drove away, I thought about the compliment he'd given me and smiled. Even if I couldn't focus for long at a time, thanks to Ross I'd given the police a new lead. Maybe I was cut out for this detective stuff after all. Leigh Dennison, armchair detective, had just entered the realm of active investigator.

Lt. Green would be proud.

From behind, I heard a soft cough. I straightened and turned to Ross and Preacher. "Yes?"

"What do we do now?" Ross asked.

I shrugged. "Just wait, I guess." I glanced down at the dogs who sat at my feet. "I think I'll just mosey on up to the house. See you later."

"Mosey?" Preacher's whispered word sounded behind me as I sauntered toward the house, the dogs trotting alongside me. I glanced back at Ross and Preacher who stared after me.

"They don't understand how I feel," I said as I opened the door and the dogs entered. "Detective Sawyer said I was a good detective."

Red growled, and I laughed. "Well, maybe those weren't his exact words, but I know that's what he meant."

The image of Clint Eastwood standing in a western street, a poncho covering his body, his hand poised to draw the pistol on his low hanging gunbelt, came to my mind. I stepped into the house and pursed my lips to whistle the haunting theme from *A Fistful of Dollars*. I only succeeded in blowing a breath of air across my lips.

Red and Jimbo stopped in the laundry room and sat on their haunches. They stared up at me as if they thought I'd lost my mind.

"I guess I need to work on that," I said to the dogs. I leaned against the washer and pretended to draw a pistol from my imaginary gunbelt. Perhaps the police were on their way to Celeste's kennel now. What I wouldn't give to see her face when she answered the door. I pointed my make-believe gun toward the kitchen and clenched my teeth like I'd seen Clint Eastwood do in so many movies. "Maybe I can't whistle, Celeste, but the police are about to call you out for a showdown."

A growl from Red brought me back to reality. I

couldn't stand around waiting for a phone call. It could take hours for the police to contact me, and I had to keep busy.

Two baskets of dirty clothes sat on the laundry room floor. The overflowing containers reminded me that it had been days since I'd washed anything. I picked up the first basket I'd brought from upstairs and began to sort the clothing into piles.

Whites here, colors over there, wash and wear between them.

When I'd finished, I did the same with the second basket. Within minutes the laundry room floor was covered with dirty clothes—at least three loads if not more. No problem. I'd get right on this job and finish in no time.

There was really no secret involved in doing laundry. A plan—that's all you needed, and I had one. Wash the first load, and while it was tumbling in the dryer, put the second load in and so on until I'd completed my task. It felt good to be so organized.

Whites first, I thought as I bent to pick up a pile. The clothes dropped back to the floor as Jimbo barked. I stepped into the kitchen where the dogs stood and spied his empty water bowl.

I grabbed the bowl and carried it to the sink. "Need a drink, boy?"

When I placed his bowl on the floor, I noticed Red's dry bowl and filled his also. As I watched the dogs lap their water, I suddenly realized the dryness in my mouth. A glass of iced tea would certainly taste good.

Minutes later, I ambled into the study, the cold drink in my hand, and sat down behind the desk. Some bills caught my attention, and I reached for them. The due date had already passed. I had to get those checks in the mail right away. Laundry would have to wait for a few minutes.

When I'd finished placing my checks in envelopes, I motioned for the dogs and headed to the front door. "The mailman hasn't gotten here yet. Let's get these to the mailbox."

My cell phone rang as I stepped off the porch, and I flipped it open. "Hello."

"Miss Dennison, this is John Sawyer."

I stood in the driveway, my heart racing. "Did they find Astro?"

"I'm afraid not."

I kicked at a rock lying next to my foot. "What happened?"

"The sheriff at Macon Falls said they went to Celeste's home and knocked on the door. No one answered. They were about to leave when an employee—a George Daniels—came around the side of the house."

"Yes, I know George. He's worked for the family for years."

"The sheriff said when they told Mr. Daniels why they were there, he assured them that all the dogs in the kennel belonged to the Witheringtons, but he wouldn't let them look around until he called Mr. Witherington."

"Did he say where Perry is?"

"New York. He told Mr. Daniels to let the police look anywhere they wanted. Mr. Daniels then took them through the three buildings that make up the kennel. There wasn't a puppy the age of Astro anywhere. The officers searched the entire property and didn't find anything."

My hand gripped the phone tighter. "I was afraid of this."

"I'm sorry, Miss Dennison," Detective Sawyer said. "The sheriff will keep an eye out on the Witheringtons. If they see anything the least bit suspicious, they'll follow up on it."

"Thank you. I appreciate all you've done."

I closed the phone and stood in the front yard wondering what I should do. The roar of a truck motor caught my attention, and I looked over my shoulder at Ross's truck coming around the corner of the house.

Ross pulled up beside me. "Have you heard anything?"

"Yes. Astro wasn't there."

From the passenger seat, Preacher leaned forward to exchange a quick glance with Ross. "They must have him hidden somewhere," Ross said. "What now?"

"I don't know."

Ross leaned out the open window of the truck. "It's almost lunchtime. I need to check on my mother, so I thought if you didn't mind, I'd go into town and see that she's all right, then grab a bite. Preacher's gonna go with me."

Nothing seemed to matter anymore. "Go on. I'll see you later."

"We won't be gone long. When we get back, we'll try to plan our next step. Okay?"

"Okay." I remembered the bills in my hand. "Would you mind putting these in the mailbox on your way?"

Ross reached for them. "No problem."

I watched them drive away and wondered if there was a next step. I had failed at so many things. I had lost my shop, I couldn't recognize the difference between a pet and a show dog, and I hadn't found Addie's killer. I'd believed Marcie and Blake when they said I was smart, but now I knew I wasn't. I was just a nice girl with ADD, and I would never succeed at anything.

"Whatever made me think I could be a detective?"

17

A feeling of shame overwhelmed me as I watched the truck disappear down the driveway. How could I have been so blind to the good traits Addie had seen in Ross and Preacher? Even after the way I'd treated them, they had been nothing but kind to me since they'd been back at the kennel. I was going to have to find a way to repay them for misjudging them.

I glanced down at the dogs standing beside me and sighed. "Well, boys, I suppose we'd better get that laundry done."

As if they understood every word, the dogs bounded up the steps ahead of me and waited at the door. The ring of my cell phone startled me, and I pulled it from my pocket. Marcie's number came up on the caller ID.

I sank down in one of the wicker chairs on the porch and flipped the phone open. "Hi, Marcie. Where have you been? I haven't heard from you in a few days."

There was a pause. "Sorry. I've just been busy. How are you?"

"Not so good right now."

For the next few minutes, I told her everything that had happened since the imposter's discovery to the search at Celeste Witherington's kennel. "Detective Sawyer said he's sure that the police over at Macon Falls will keep a close watch on the Witheringtons. If they do anything suspicious, the police will be on them right away."

Marcie clucked her disapproval. "I'm sure John is right about the police watching the Witheringtons."

Something in her voice made me sit up straighter. I know it shouldn't bother me, but I felt rather irritated that my best friend referred to him on a first-name basis, seeing as how I'd considered him an adversary just a few days ago. "Must you refer to Detective Sawyer on a first-name basis?"

Marcie sighed. "I don't want you to be upset with me, Leigh. I know you and John didn't get off to a good start, but he really is a nice guy."

I had to admit Marcie was right. After all, he had been very nice to me when I went to the police station, and he had helped me overcome my suspicions of Blake. Maybe if I concentrated hard enough, I could come to like him. "I've found that out."

"Well, he called me after he came to the shop that day—you know when he questioned you. And he said he'd like to get to know me better. We've been out several times."

I could hear the conflict she must be experiencing in her voice. She didn't want to be disloyal to a friend, but I knew she liked John. Marcie was the best friend I'd ever had, and I wanted her to be happy.

I smiled and relaxed in the chair. "Marcie, you don't have to worry about me. All I want is your happiness. If you want to go out with John Sawyer, then you have my blessing."

"Really?"

"Yeah. You're right. He is a nice guy. I misjudged him." I thought of Ross, Preacher, and Blake. "Like I have so many other people. I think Addie would be proud that I'm finally learning what she tried to teach me—that we need to be more concerned about those around us."

"Leigh, you don't know how glad I am to hear you say this. John said he'd like for you and Blake to go out to dinner with us. Would you do that?"

"Sure. Blake's out of town, but he'll be home soon. Then we'll plan it."

"I can hardly wait." Excitement brightened Marcie's voice. "You're really going to like John."

"I'm sure I will."

After we said our good-byes I closed my phone and sat there thinking about Marcie and John. Maybe things were looking up for Marcie and me. We'd often wondered if we would ever find the right guys, and now maybe we both had.

Guilt welled up in me at the thought of Blake. I hoped he never found out that I had suspected him of Addie's murder. That might destroy any chance of a relationship.

I stood up from the chair and pointed my finger at the dogs. "Don't you two ever utter one word." They cocked their heads and stared at me. I laughed and opened the front door. "Come on, let's get some lunch."

Thirty minutes later, I sat at the kitchen table, the remnants of my half-eaten turkey sandwich in front of me. I couldn't eat for thinking of a killer still at large. I pushed back from the table, crossed my arms, and began to pace around the room.

Anger boiled up in me. "I can't believe the police didn't find anything."

Red and Jimbo gazed up at me then settled back down.

I glanced into the laundry room and groaned at the sight of the dirty clothes still on the floor. *No time to think about laundry now.*

I pressed my fists to my temples in frustration. "I've got to do something. But what?"

No answer came, and I strode back across the room. I stopped and gazed out the window over the sink toward the kennel. I'd never felt so helpless in my life. "I wish Ross and Preacher would get back so we can talk about our next move."

Until then, I needed to find something to occupy my mind.

My empty coffee cup still sat beside my plate at the table. I remembered I'd poured the last of the grounds into the coffeemaker before lunch. It dawned on me what I could do to pass the time until Ross and Preacher returned. "I'll make my grocery list, and then I've got to do that laundry."

The dogs jumped to their feet at that moment and

began to bark. "What is it, fellows?"

A knock on the front door sent them running through the house with me hurrying behind. I pulled the door open and blinked in astonishment at George Daniels standing on my front porch. Instead of the work clothes I'd seen him in before, he wore khaki pants with a shirt and tie. There was no mistaking the worried expression on his face.

"Mr. Daniels, what a surprise. What are you doing here?"

His weathered brow wrinkled. "Oh, Miss Dennison, I'm so upset. I feel like I need to talk to you."

The man was clearly distressed. "Are you all right?"

He closed his eyes and rubbed his hand across his forehead. "Yes, I'm fine. It's such a warm day. I think I got too hot."

"Come in, and let me get you some water." I pushed the door open.

He followed me through the house and into the kitchen. Once there he eased into a chair at the table. When I set the water in front of him, his hand shook as he raised the glass to his mouth. After a few sips his hands grew steadier.

"I'm sorry to be such a bother. I don't know what happened to me."

I leaned down and studied him carefully. His cheeks had a rosy tint, and his breathing appeared regular. His eyes seemed clearer than I had at first thought. "Why were you so upset?"

His lips twitched, and he bit down on the lower

one. "The police came to our kennel today."

"Yes, I know." The smell of the coffee caught my attention. "Would you like a cup of coffee?"

He smiled. "That would be nice. That is if it's not any trouble."

"None at all. I've already got it made."

Red and Jimbo entered the kitchen and settled in their usual corner of the room. They glanced up as I poured the coffee, then lay back down.

"Cream or sugar?" I asked.

"No, black is fine."

I brought the cups to the table and settled in a chair across from George. We stirred our coffee in silence. After a few moments, I glanced up at him. "Detective Sawyer from St. Claire called and told me you allowed the police to search Celeste's kennel."

"Mr. Perry told me to. Said he didn't have anything to hide."

I didn't know what to say because I still believed that Celeste had Astro hidden somewhere. I took a sip from my cup. "Well, after we discovered that the puppy I have is not Astro, it seemed the logical place to look for him would be in a kennel that raises the same kind of dogs."

He tipped his head up and looked thoughtful before he answered. "I suppose so, but Mr. Perry would never allow anything like that to happen."

I glanced down at the table. "Well, time will tell."

His eyes narrowed, and the muscle in his jaw twitched. "Your suspicions of Celeste and Mr. Perry are unfounded."

He was getting upset again, and I didn't want to cause him anymore distress, so I smiled. "The Witheringtons are very fortunate to have such a loyal employee."

George's shoulders relaxed some, and he smiled back at me. "Like I told you before, I worked for Mr. Perry's father, and I owe him a lot."

I reached across and squeezed his hand. "And I'm sure Celeste and Perry appreciate that. I hope someday I'll be able to produce the same loyalty in my employees."

He regarded me with serious eyes. "So you're still planning to run the kennel."

"Oh yes. With or without Astro we're going right ahead. We may not ever breed another potential Westminster winner, but we'll do okay. Ross and Preacher are going to help me, and one of Addie's friends from Atlanta will give me all the advice I need."

"I see." He glanced at his watch and pushed his chair back. "Oh my, I didn't realize the time. I've got a lot to do at home, so I'd better be going."

I stood up and faced him. "Thanks for coming, George. I'll look forward to seeing you again soon."

He stared at me for a moment. "Think about what you're going to do. I've been working with dogs for years, and I know how difficult it can be. You're a nice girl, and I just hate to see you get into something that can be so overwhelming to a beginner."

"Thanks, George. I'll remember your advice."

"Especially when you could do many other things. I know your antique shop burned, but somebody told me you can build furniture."

"I've produced some that I thought was quite good."

He smiled. "See, you've got a business right there. No telling what the tourists in town would pay for a mountain-made piece."

I laughed. "Oh, I don't know. I'm not that good."

"I'll bet you could do a big business. You've already got all the tools you need in your workshop. You could get started right away."

I picked up our cups from the table and turned to set them on the cabinet. "I don't know, I. . ." The cups rattled in my hand, and I eased them down on the counter. I turned to face him. "How do you know what I've got in my workshop? The day you came here with Perry you told me you had never been here before."

The lines in his face tightened as he grimaced. He pushed his chair up to the table and took a step toward me. "I'm sorry you remembered that."

I backed away, pulling my chair out as a barrier between us. The truth suddenly hit me. He could only have been in my shop if he was looking for a weapon to kill Addie.

"You," I whispered. "You were the one. But why? She never did anything to hurt you."

George stood there for a moment, his breath coming in short spurts and his eyes wide. Then he took a deep breath, and it was as if a transformation occurred in his body. His eyebrows drew down across the bridge of his nose, and he bit his bottom lip. All pretense of distress was gone from his face. Too late, I realized I'd been deceived.

He moved toward me. "Well, little miss detective, you think you've solved a mystery, do you? What do you think you're going to do about it?"

I took a step back, pulling the chair with me. "I'm going to tell the police."

His eyes glowered at me, and he shook his head. "Oh no, you're not. You're not going to ruin everything Mr. Perry and I have worked for."

"Perry knows you killed Addie?"

He laughed. "Of course not."

Maybe if I could stall him long enough I could find a way to escape, but first I had to get a confession. My gaze darted about the room. *About fifteen steps to the door.* Could I make it? I inched in that direction. "Did he find out you'd stolen Astro?"

He advanced another step, and I retreated, the chair still between us. "It was that stupid Celeste. She switched the dogs. I told her she had to take Astro back, but she refused. So I put the dog in the truck and came to bring him back."

My throat ached with fear, but I had to find out more. *Keep him talking.* "What happened then?"

"I thought I might be able to sneak in and exchange the dogs before Mrs. Jordan found out. But when I drove up, she was coming out of the kennel. I told her she could have the dog back and that I'd keep a watch on Celeste. But she wouldn't listen to me. She said she was going to call the police and ran toward the house. I couldn't let her ruin Mr. Perry's business.

I remembered Celeste telling me about your workshop being next to the kennel, and I ran over to it. The door was unlocked, and I grabbed the first thing I saw."

Oh, why didn't I lock that door?

"I followed Mrs. Jordan to the house. She had her back turned to me and was just picking up the phone when I entered. She never heard me until I stabbed her in the back."

The pain Addie must have suffered brought tears to my eyes, but I had to know more. "But why did you take the deposit?"

"To make it look like a robbery, of course. I saw the bag on her desk, and I didn't want anybody to look too closely at the puppy."

I took another step. *Thirteen more to the door.* "But the check in the truck? How did you do that?"

He laughed. "I heard in town that you thought that boy had killed Addie. I came by one day when no one was here and put it under the front seat of the truck. I thought that would point suspicions toward him."

I shook my head. "But I don't understand why you let Perry keep trying to buy the imposter back."

"Oh, come on, Leigh. You're smarter than that. If you had sold us the puppy, I would have been in the clear. No one would have ever known about the switch and connected me to the murder. You could have saved yourself a lot of grief if you'd just given up, but no, you had to be some kind of hero."

I glanced around for a weapon. A frying pan sat on

the counter, but my chair and George blocked the way. "Wh–what do you mean?"

"I decided that I'd have to get rid of the imposter if you weren't going to sell him to Mr. Perry. So I came over to burn the kennel, but he wasn't there."

I sucked in my breath. George—the last person I would have suspected. "The puppy was in the house with me."

"Oh, he was? Well, I should have set your house on fire instead of burning down your shop."

My fingers tightened on the back of the chair. "You were the arsonist? But why?"

"After I couldn't find the puppy, I thought I'd set fire to the antique shop. I hoped that would distract you from trying to solve the murder and then you might sell the puppy. But you just wouldn't give up, would you?"

"B–but I saw Perry at the fire. Why was he there?"

"He'd been on a trip and was on his way home when he saw the fire's glow. He stopped by to see what was burning." George chuckled. "I was properly sad the next morning when he told me about your misfortune."

The knife drawer was right behind me. If I could get it open, I'd have a weapon. I scooted closer so I could make my move.

A low growl came from the direction of the dogs. Out of the corner of my eye, I saw that Red and Jimbo were on their feet, their teeth bared. "No! Don't tell me anymore. I can't stand to hear this. Save it for the police after they've arrested you." George's eyes narrowed. "I don't think I'll tell them anything." His fingers fumbled with the knot of his tie, and then he slowly pulled it from around his neck. He looped the ends over both his hands and pulled the tie taut.

I stared at him in disbelief. "I–I'll tell them everything you've told me."

"And just how do you think you're going to do that?" He pressed closer to me.

"You can't scare me." I whirled toward the knife drawer and reached for the handle.

My head jerked back as George's tie looped around my neck and tightened. I let go of the drawer and clawed at my throat, but it was no use. George pulled me backwards as he choked the breath from me.

He leaned forward and whispered in my ear. "You'd better be afraid of me, because my face is the last one you're ever going to see."

18

I struggled to free myself, but he pulled me backward. My feet lifted from the floor. Even with our age difference, his strength far surpassed mine, but I continued to struggle. I gasped for breath and tried to punch him in the ribs with my elbows.

Just as I thought I could fight him no longer, a howl followed by a shrill bark erupted. In an instant Red and Jimbo, their barks filling the air, were beside me.

"Let go," George yelled, and his fingers loosened.

I reached over my shoulder and clawed at his face, and he stumbled away from me. I straightened, pulled the tie from my throat, and cupped my throbbing neck. Jimbo, growling and shaking like a perpetual motion machine, had one of George's pants legs clenched in his teeth. George tried to kick at the puppy, but Jimbo pulled that much harder.

Red grabbed the other pant leg and pulled in the opposite direction. George swatted at both dogs as he tried to free himself from their clenched jaws.

"Get away!" he yelled, but the dogs hung on as if their lives depended on it.

Freed from his grip, I grabbed the cell phone from my pocket and dialed 911. Before the dispatcher could finish his speech, I was screaming in his ear. "This is Leigh Dennison at Jordan's Kennels. George Daniels just tried to kill me. Send some officers right away."

"Is the perpetrator still there?" the voice asked.

George hopped across the floor toward the laundry room trying to free himself, but it was no use.

"He's still here. Please hurry."

"I've dispatched officers. There's a car in the area. They should be there in a few minutes. Stay on the phone with me until they arrive."

"All right. My dogs have him cornered right now, but he may get away."

As if on cue, Red let go of George's leg and jumped on him, pushing him backward.

The officer's voice came back on the phone. "Get yourself to safety, ma'am, until the officers arrive."

My gaze settled on the frying pan, and I grabbed it. I advanced on George who was still fighting at the dogs.

George stood in the laundry room, one foot in the pile of whites and the other in the wash and wear. He twisted and turned trying to free himself, but his feet became entangled in the dirty clothes. Red lunged, and his front paws struck George in the stomach. George tried to kick, but his feet began to slide in different directions. He looked like an acrobat doing the splits in slow motion.

Jimbo gave one last tug, and with a thud, George toppled backward to the floor. Red stood over him as if daring him to move. Jimbo joined the big bloodhound, and they snarled every time George attempted to rise.

George pushed up on his elbows and glared at me. I looked down at him and raised the frying pan over my head. "Just make one move, George, and you'll wish you hadn't."

Sirens pierced the air, and I put the cell phone back to my ear and spoke to the dispatcher. "The police are here. Tell them the front door is unlocked. They'll find us in the kitchen."

After a moment, the dispatcher's voice sounded in my ear. "I've told them. They're on the way in. Are you sure you're okay?"

The front door banged open, and footsteps sounded in the hall. "Police!"

"Ma'am," the voice on the phone said. "Are you okay?"

I glanced down at George where he still lay with the two dogs standing over him and smiled.

"That's a 10/4. I've never been better."

Hours later Marcie, Preacher, and Ross sat with me in the living room of the house. Jimbo and Red lay on the floor at my feet. From time to time, I reached down to pat my two heroes. Every time I did, they rewarded me with a lick on the hand. I had never felt more at peace.

"Leigh, I'll see if I can rustle up something for everybody to eat." Marcie's words reminded me that I'd had nothing since the half-eaten turkey sandwich.

I rose to follow her to the kitchen. "I'll help you." Ross and Preacher stood and blocked my exit.

"No, you just take it easy. We're gonna take care of you tonight." Ross pointed to the sofa, and I sat down

I pushed a pillow behind me and settled back. "You don't have to treat me like an invalid."

Preacher stared at me. "Miss Leigh, that man almost killed you."

I looked from Ross to Preacher and smiled. "But he didn't, thanks to the dogs."

Preacher leaned down and patted Jimbo. "They sure are mighty fine dogs."

Ross and Preacher settled in chairs across from me, and I was overcome by the concern on their faces. I sat there in the quiet room, thinking of Addie and how she ministered to these two, and I wondered if I could ever be like her. I wanted to be, and I said a silent prayer of thanks for her life and what she meant to me.

I took a deep breath and glanced at Ross. "I want to apologize again to you for thinking you killed Addie. I'm afraid I've been unkind to you in the past, but I want to make it up to you."

"Miss Leigh, you don't have to explain. I've faced that kind of treatment all my life."

"Well, it's time we did something about it. I want you to work here whether or not we get Astro back. There will be other puppies, and we'll train them and show them together. That is if you still want the job."

His face brightened with a huge smile. "Oh, Miss Leigh, nothing would make me happier."

"There is one stipulation, though."

Wariness crept into his eyes. "What is it?"

"I want you to go back to school and get your high school diploma. I suppose, though, it'll have to be a GED since you're already over eighteen. After that, we'll talk about college if you're interested in going on."

A look of surprise flashed across his face. "I can't go back to school. The GED classes meet at night. If I work here during the day and go to school at night, who'll take care of my mother when I'm in class?"

"I will. We'll work together to train the dogs and take care of your mother, too."

A look of total wonder filled his face. "You'd do that for me?" Then he shook his head. "No, that's too much for you to take on."

"No it isn't. Especially if my other helper will pitch in."

"What other helper?"

I turned to Preacher. "I want you to forgive me, too. When I found out you had Addie's Bible, I felt sure you had killed her. And I treated you so awful when Addie was alive. I want to make it up to you. Would you like to help us with the dogs? You can work with Ross and cover for him when he's in class and help me with whatever I need around the farm."

Preacher's eyes grew wide, and I thought I detected a tear in the corners. "You want me to work here, too?"

"Yes, I do."

A smile spread across his face. "I'd like that. Ever since I got here, I've wished it'd work out for me to settle down. I guess I'll just make that bridge my permanent home."

I shook my head. "No. You're not staying under that bridge another night. There's an apartment over my workshop, and you're moving in there today. It needs a good cleaning, but we'll fix it up for you."

The tear I thought I'd seen spilled out of his eye and trickled down his cheek. "It's been a long time since I slept indoors. I don't rightly know how it'll feel."

I looked from Ross to Preacher, and happiness bubbled up inside of me. Maybe at last I had learned what Addie had tried to teach me. I had lost her, and the man who had killed her had also taken away my beloved antique shop. But deep in my heart I knew I'd found a sense of love that could heal all the hurts the world might throw at me. I thought Addie would be pleased with how I finally understood what drove her to show love to all around her.

"Good, then everything's settled."

Jimbo stood up at that moment and pawed at my leg. I scooped up the puppy and held him close. This dog would always be special to me. George Daniels had no regard for him either and wanted to kill him just as he had Addie. Jimbo licked at my face, and I laughed as I tried to hold the squirming body.

Marcie, carrying a tray loaded with ham sandwiches and Cokes, walked into the room and set it on the coffee table. She glanced down, a smile curling her lips at the excitement of the puppy.

"He's so cute."

A sudden thought caused me to sit up straight. "Marcie, he doesn't really belong to me. Do you think

I'll be able to keep him?"

"Why don't we save all our questions for the police? George is in jail, and they're on the lookout for Celeste. Maybe we'll know something soon." She motioned to the tray of food. "Dig in everybody. I would have fixed something a little fancier, but we all know Leigh's no cook, so there wasn't much to choose from in the kitchen." We all laughed as we reached for the food. For the next few minutes we ate and discussed the events of the day.

Preacher swallowed a big bite and washed it down with a swig of Coke before he spoke up. "I shore would've liked to see Miss Leigh standing over that fellow with that frying pan. We best watch out in the future, Ross."

We laughed, and I took another bite just as a knock sounded at the front door.

Marcie jumped up. "I'll get it. Maybe that's John now."

When she walked back into the room, John accompanied her. I looked at the two of them together and wondered why I had ever disliked the handsome, young police detective. Maybe it was the way he and Marcie looked at each other. Or maybe it was my feelings for Blake. Whatever the reason, I knew at that moment that Marcie and I had both found the men we had been searching for since high school. I smothered a giggle as I thought how the two of them almost looked like the men we used to describe to each other.

John walked toward me, a smile on his face. "I

have some good news for you, Leigh."

I stood, my heart racing. "What is it?"

"We put out a bulletin on Celeste's car. I just got a call that she'd been stopped on I-40 headed toward Knoxville. She's been taken into custody and will be returned to our county tomorrow."

I let out a long breath. "That's good news. What will she be charged with?"

"Robbery, transporting stolen goods across state lines, and maybe accomplice to murder. She must have known what George did but kept quiet about it."

I thought back to what George had told me. "George said they had Astro with a trainer in Knoxville."

John nodded. "She was on her way there. She hoped no one would find out about his whereabouts for a few days. This trainer has contacts in England, and she'd made arrangements with him to send the dog there."

"I can't believe she and George went to such lengths, but I suppose they were in a panic to cover their tracks."

John smiled. "Yeah, or George never would have come here today. It's a good thing he did, though. We might never have found out the truth." He paused for a moment. "Thanks for your help in catching him, Leigh."

My face grew warm at the compliment. John wasn't such a bad guy after all. "You're welcome, but there's still the matter of Perry. Do you really think he knew nothing about all this?"

John's forehead wrinkled as if in deep thought. "We got in touch with Perry in New York. He was shocked at what we told him. He said he came back to run his father's business so he could keep an eye on his stepmother, but he had no idea about George's involvement in the murder. He's given us his alibi on the day of the murder, and we'll check it out. But George also said Perry had nothing to do with it."

I remembered how protective George had been of Perry. "George is very loyal to Perry because of his father."

"I think Perry's just been trying to get the business profitable again. He says he had no idea about the switch. In fact I don't think he even likes dogs much."

"I could tell their animals weren't very well cared for the day I went over there."

"We've contacted the Humane Society, and they've gone out to Celeste's kennel. From what they told me about the conditions there, I think Perry Witherington got to North Carolina a little too late to save his business. When I talked with him, he indicated he's coming back here just long enough to put the business up for sale. He said he'd cooperate with us any way he can."

I breathed a sigh of relief. "You're just full of good news. Addie's murderer has been caught, and Perry Witherington won't be around anymore."

John stepped close and put his hand on my shoulder. "I want to offer my congratulations to you for figuring out what happened. Getting George to confess was a good piece of detective work."

Maybe he was worthy of Marcie after all. "I appreciate that, John." A sudden thought popped into my head. "What about Astro?"

John laughed. "He's having a great time with the Knoxville police. We'll get him in the morning, too, unless you want to drive over and pick him up yourself."

I shook my head. "No, that's okay. Are they sure he's all right?"

"The captain over there told me they're going to take him to a vet and have him checked out, but they think he's fine. He'll probably spend the night there."

"I can go get him, Miss Leigh, if you want," Ross interrupted.

"No," I said. "We'll let John bring him back tomorrow."

Ross smiled. "Well, I think I'll go help Preacher move his stuff from the bridge to the apartment. Then I need to get home. I'll see you in the morning."

"See you," I said as I followed the two of them to the door. "We have a lot of work ahead of us. Astro's coming home."

When I turned to reenter the den, I almost laughed at the baffled look on Marcie's face. "Apartment? What's he talking about?"

"I'll tell you later," I whispered.

We walked back toward the couch, but I stopped in amazement. Red and Jimbo lay curled up in the corner of the room as if they were oblivious to all the comings and goings of the last few minutes—not at all like they'd been earlier with George. Jimbo's head rested on Red's outstretched paw, and I thought I could almost hear contented snores coming from their direction.

"Get a look at that, John. Jimbo feels at home here. Will I be able to keep him?"

He shrugged. "I don't think there'll be any problem. Celeste is in no position to object."

"Well, I for one am glad this case is over," Marcie interrupted. "Maybe Leigh will give up her idea of solving crimes and things will get back to normal around here."

John smiled and turned toward Marcie. "Maybe so." He winked. "Are you ready to go? If you are, I'll follow you home."

Marcie picked up the tray with our leftover food on it. "Let me take this to the kitchen, and I'll be right back."

John watched her go then turned back to me. "I imagine you'll sleep better tonight knowing you've helped catch a murderer. The police are always glad to have the support of citizens in the community."

"Thanks, I. . ." I stopped in mid-sentence and looked at him. "Tell me, John. Has the mayor ever thought about starting a citizens' police academy?"

His eyes widened. "I don't think so. Why?"

"Oh, no reason. Just a thought." Marcie came back into the room, and I followed them to the front door. With a smile, I waved good-bye before I closed the door and leaned against it. "A citizens' police academy.

Maybe that's what St. Claire needs. I'll get started on that tomorrow."

My cell phone rang, and I pulled it from my pocket. The number on the caller ID thrilled me. "Hi, Blake."

"Leigh, what's going on there? I had a voice mail from Marcie that I needed to call you. Are you all right?"

"I'm fine. When are you coming home?"

"Tomorrow. But what's happened?"

"Well, Blake," I began, "I suppose I should tell you how Red, Jimbo, and I caught a murderer today."

Two nights later Blake and I drove home after having dinner with Marcie and John. Although I'd had doubts about the evening, I had enjoyed it. I smiled as I thought of how happy Marcie had looked.

"I think John and Marcie really like each other." Blake's words broke the comfortable silence between us.

"Um, I guess so." Marcie had never looked happier than she did during the time we'd spent together.

Blake glanced over at me. "And you're all right about their seeing each other?"

I sat silent for a moment. I had certainly learned a lot in the last few weeks. "I'm fine. I just want Marcie to be happy."

"Yeah." For a few minutes he didn't say anything. "What did you mean when you asked John if he'd thought about your suggestion?"

"Oh, it was just a thought I had."

He eased up on the accelerator and glanced over at me. "Okay, tell me what you're cooking up in that brain of yours now."

I reached down and adjusted my seat belt. "Why whatever do you mean?"

"Leigh, I can tell you're up to something."

There was plenty of time to tell him about my idea. It would be better if I waited a few days until the scare over my adventure had calmed down a little. And besides I would need Blake and Marcie's help to convince the mayor and police department of my plan.

We were going to have a great time being trained as volunteer policemen. I could just see us searching deserted buildings in hopes of finding hidden stolen property, booking and fingerprinting prisoners at the jail, or making a citizen's arrest. Maybe they'd even let us drive a squad car. But I'd tell Blake all that later.

Blake turned the truck into the entrance to the farm and guided it to a stop in front of the house. He turned off the motor, hopped out, and came around to help me out. We stopped on the porch, and I turned to him.

"I had a wonderful time tonight, Blake."

He gazed into my eyes and put his arms around me. "Leigh, I told you we needed to have a talk when I got back. I've been trying, but something always gets in the way."

My breath caught in my throat. "It has been busy, but we're alone now."

He smiled. "I've been trying to tell you I've fallen in love with you." He swallowed before continuing. "You're the best thing that's ever happened to me, and I hope you have the same feelings for me."

My heart felt like it could soar to the sky, but for once, I concentrated on the moment. My arms circled his neck. "I love you, too, Blake Cameron." He pulled me closer, but I drew back. "You're not worried about my ADD?"

"What ADD?" he whispered. "A smart girl like you and a nice guy like me—I think we're made for each other."

I smiled up into his handsome face. "I'll warn you again before it's too late. You'd better buckle your seat belt and put your chair back, tray in the upright and locked position. You may be in for a bumpy flight."

His lips moved closer to mine. "Or the ride of a lifetime."

Sandra Robbins, a former teacher and principal in the Tennessee public schools, is a full-time writer and adjunct college professor. She is married to her college sweetheart, and they have four children and five grandchildren. As a child, Sandra accepted Jesus as her Savior and has depended on Him to guide her throughout her life.

She is active in her church where she plays the organ and directs the handbell choir.

While working as a principal, Sandra came in contact with many individuals who were so burdened with problems that they found it difficult to function in their everyday lives. Her writing ministry grew out of the need for hope that she saw in the lives of those around her.

It is her prayer that God will use her words to plant seeds of hope in the lives of her readers. Her greatest desire is that many will come to know the peace she draws from her life verse, Isaiah 40:31—"But those who hope in the LORD will renew their strength. They will soar on wings like eagles; they will run and not grow weary, they will walk and not be faint."

You may correspond with this author by writing:
Sandra Robbins
Author Relations
PO Box 721
Uhrichsville, OH 44683

A Letter to Our Readers

Dear Reader:

In order to help us satisfy your quest for more great mystery stories, we would appreciate it if you would take a few minutes to respond to the following questions. We welcome your comments and read each form and letter we receive. When completed, please return to:

Fiction Editor
Heartsong Presents—MYSTERIES!
PO Box 721
Uhrichsville, Ohio 44683

Did you enjoy reading *Pedigreed Bloodlines* by Sandra Robbins?

☐ Very much! I would like to see more books like this!
The one thing I particularly enjoyed about this story was:

_____

_____

_____

☐ Moderately. I would have enjoyed it more if:

_____

_____

_____

Are you a member of the HP—MYSTERIES! Book Club?
☐ Yes ☐ No

If no, where did you purchase this book?

_____

Please rate the following elements using a scale of 1 (poor) to 10 (superior):

___ Main character/sleuth   ___ Romance elements

___ Inspirational theme   ___ Secondary characters

___ Setting   ___ Mystery plot

How would you rate the cover design on a scale of 1 (poor) to 5 (superior)? _____

What themes/settings would you like to see in future **Heartsong Presents—MYSTERIES!** selections? _____
_____
_____
_____

Please check your age range:
- ◯ Under 18
- ◯ 18–24
- ◯ 25–34
- ◯ 35–45
- ◯ 46–55
- ◯ Over 55

Name: _____

Occupation: _____

Address: _____

E-mail address: _____

┌Heartsong Presents—MYSTERIES!┐

Any 8 Titles for $32! A 20% Savings!

Great Mysteries at a Great Price! Purchase Any Title for Only $4.97 Each!

HEARTSONG PRESENTS—MYSTERIES! TITLES AVAILABLE NOW:

Heartsong Presents—MYSTERIES! provide romance and faith interwoven among the pages of these fun whodunits. Written by the talented and brightest authors in this genre, such as Christine Lynxwiler, Cecil Murphey, Nancy Mehl, Dana Mentink, Candice Speare, and many others, these cozy tales are sure to challenge your mind, warm your heart, touch your spirit—and put your sleuthing skills to the test.

Not all titles may be available at time of order.
If outside the U.S., please call
740-922-7280 for shipping charges.

SEND TO: **Heartsong Presents—Mysteries! Readers' Service**
P.O. Box 721, Uhrichsville, Ohio 44683

Please send me the items checked above. I am enclosing $_____
(please add $3.00 to cover postage per order. OH add 7% tax. WA add 8.5%). Send check or money order—no cash or C.O.D.s, please.

To place a credit card order, call 1-740-922-7280.

NAME _____

ADDRESS _____

CITY/STATE _____ ZIP_____

OHIO
Weddings

3 stories in 1

Secrets, love, and danger are afoot when three remarkable women reexamine their lives on Bay Island. Lauren Wright returns to straighten out her past only to disrupt her future. Becky Merrill steps onto the shore and into sabotage. Judi Rydell can't outrun her former life. Who will rescue their hearts?

ISBN 978-1-59789-987-1
Contemporary, paperback, 352 pages, $6.97

_____

A BRIDE SO FAIR

Emily Ralston is delighted when she lands a job at the Children's Building at the World's Fair. When a lost boy is found by a handsome guard and soon after a dead body turns up, the mystery begins to unfold. Can Emily deliver little Adam to safety before time runs out?

ISBN 978-59789-492-0
288 pages, $9.97